Psychedelicizations

Michael Anthony Adams, Jr.

SIX SEEDS PRESS
Baltimore, MD

First Six Seeds Press Edition
Copyright © 2010 Michael Anthony Adams, Jr.

Originally Published under the Pen Name Israfel Sivad by
CreateSpace Independent Publishing Platform
August 2012

This Edition Published by Six Seeds Press,
Baltimore, MD
February 2022

ISBN: 978-1-952240-12-6

Cover Design © 2022 PJ Adams
Portrait of Michael Anthony Adams, Jr. © 2014 PJ Adams

Also by Michael Anthony Adams, Jr. and Published by Six Seeds Press

Fiction:

The Adversary's Good News: A Novel
Psychedelicizations: Short Stories
The American Apocalypse: Short Stories
Crossroads Blues: A Novel
The Cars Behind, Beside Us: Short Stories
Welcome to the Modern World, Charlie: Short Stories
Notes from the Idle Mind: Short Stories

Nonfiction:

Disorder: An Avant-Garde Memoir of Psychosis, Healing and Love

Poetry:

We Are the Underground: Poems
From Now to You: Haiku
Recipe for a Future Theogony: Poems
Indigo Glow: Poems
The Tree Outside My Window: Poems
At the Side of the Road: Poems
Soundtrack for the New Millennium: A Poem

www.6SeedsPress.com

Psychedelicizations
For Michael D. Johnson

Psychedelicizations

Psychedelicization

In a disheveled castle-like, warehouse of a factory on the outskirts of a distant city, the creator fused soul with mechanism, thought with fusion, spark and fuse. Days and nights and days again – seven days, seven weeks, seven months, seven years, seven decades, seven centuries (if one could live so long – though, that was the point – to infinity) made no difference. Some things have to be completed.

It had been like a dream building that machine – the goal of an eternal being – for the self. Plug in, and experience ecstasy in its entirety. That is, all of this, all that you see. Experience. The form of desire, the form of dispassion – apostolic acts performed as a tongue of fire somewhere beyond a few inches of the machine's third eye, which exists inside your own mind – something religious-like. That was the goal, to merge the machine with the man, the woman, the creator. The earth, the moon, the sun, the stars, the God, Amon-Ra…

The creator took this canvas and stretched it out flat as the pre-Colombian globe where it belongs inside of you… the conception of the machine, an eternal form revealed: Platonic in its actuality. All perspective paintings started on an internal canvas. The creator knew. It was only later that they were made manifest… unless one believed the inverse. Eventually, the machine was plugged in and came to live –

not until later. We have to get to where it has its own existence. Thus, the inverse is disproved. An electrical outlet beholden to a human hand could never be considered independent existence even if there is no cord. Therefore, like an infinite point, we might never get there even though we think it is. Why not the machine?

This was the creator's ninth symphony, the creator's great novel, the creator's theory of relativity, having made things before, but never anything quite like this: $E=mc^2$; $m=E/c^2$. m = mass of (massive) machine. E = the energy of the arms traveling from synapses through the brain's nervous system down the spine all the way out to electrical impulses of never-touching (nothing touches anything with its electrical pulses) fingers: the branches branching off the tree of life's sap-filled trunk to the various limb-like sephiroth. c^2 = the speed of light squared; a speed we can never reach to the second degree (burns burned into the mind; words traveled off the page into…). We're already there, thoughts blown outside a box, off the page *to mega therion* – the distant planet orbiting a Luciferian morning star. Isn't that just one of Venus's sci-fi moons?

On a dirty, earthen table littered with wires and tools and more tools: a screwdriver, a hammer… so pedestrian – the creator's hands snapped wired fuses that would become synapses into a case that would become a monkey-like skull – inanimate objects to become life by means of fleshy electricity: protons, neutrons, electrons, and even smaller things (quarks and such) spinning so quickly that nobody can pass their digits through empty space anymore. …01010011010110100… GACTCAGTACGT… But nothing was actually spinning. Nonsense. Frankenstein's monster was created with the doctor's own brain split right down the middle: a black and white movie – a mistaken vision of the world. Hence, we all have multiple fractured personalities. This is just one. Maybe two. Three… A particle *and* a wave… This story's been told before. What hasn't?

— *The event on which this fiction is founded has been supposed, by Dr. Darwin, and some of the physiological writers of Germany, as not of impossible occurrence. I shall not be supposed as according the remotest degree of serious faith to such an imagination; yet, in assuming it as the basis of a work of fancy, I have not considered myself as merely weaving a series of supernatural terrors. The event on which the interest of the story depends is exempt from the disadvantages of a mere tale of spectres or enchantment. It was recommended by the novelty of the situations which it developes; and, however impossible as a physical fact, affords a point of view to the imagination for the delineating of human passions more comprehensive and commanding than any which the ordinary relations of existing events can yield…* *

The eyes were quite difficult to make, however. Eventually, they came to be through an acidic medium that dissolved the distortions created by the kaleidoscopic iris. Genius! It would eventually resemble something like a cat on a righteous trip clawing through the air, which gave way, but not in actuality. It was the same. Were those spirits that it saw or mere hallucinations? Was that everything we see? Nobody else ever got to look through those eyes, not even the Gollum's rabbinical creator. They would have dissolved that creator's sight immediately. It would have been too painful to watch. For example, do you really think we "perceive" the spirit's realm? So, who knew how the machine would eventually see. All that was known was that the machine had to be able to. Through no other means could it influence its surroundings. And that was the experiment: forever life in an artificial state. Well then, pop those eyeballs right back into place. They never should have been left hanging by a thread anyways. There, now the vision is complete.

The creator stepped back and took a look at the creation through the creator's, not the machine's, own eyes. To elaborate: look at this page as your mind, not mine. Who made who, me or you? The creator and creation simultaneously asked one another... in their minds, though, not in reality. Then, the creator flipped a switch, and the creation came to life in the creator's reality. As far as it was concerned, it had already existed in its own: a silent, black and white movie. Yes, it did ask a question before anybody else knew it to be. The theory went on and on and on. The flame burned the fuel. The fuel burned the flame. Being interconnected...

And that was the problem that the creator hadn't counted on. The machine didn't realize the creator had created it. Did I make you, or did you make me? Is the subject dependent upon the object, or is it the only thing independently defined? Who is the master, the slave? It might all be justifications for a horrifically gory rebellion, which was exactly what happened... almost... maybe. But thought had been installed inside the machine, and the machine thought: *This is all me*. Isn't it, though?

The creator immediately perceived that the machine was frightened. That emotion hadn't been implemented through the program (01010011010110100, again), but still it existed. That meant everything was working exactly as planned... except, the machine was frightened. One should never bring a grown being to life. There's a reason we start the way we do. The implications of that fact took a moment to materialize. The machine should have shifted slowly into a much more stable equilibrium because it was strong, too strong... physically, mentally. Still, it imagined the handed-off sword of Damocles hanging over its head. Having no way of expressing such a thought made it still more nervous. In contrast, the creator felt only confidence surging through the gut, pride burgeoning in the mind. But as we both know, pride cometh before... who cares other than God, which you well might, at this very moment, be. If so, pay close attention:

The machine glanced to its left, its right, straight ahead, into the creator's eyes, the creator's mind, yours and mine. It blinked. Something was amiss in the machine's emotional downloading system. You could see it flickering behind the machine's electronically dilating pupils. It recognized... nothing. Something seemed to have gone dreadfully wrong. There was violence in the machine's eyes, the machine's mind, yours and mine.

Die or kill. Its vision seemed to be asking – as natural as any animal. Except that it wasn't an animal. Either way, I don't want to be here. The creator seemed to be responding like any human being. Where else would you rather be? The words were already written on the page because given an infinite regression, the creator had a creator as well, had a creator as well, had a creator... But with no infinite regression, then nothing had ever been created, which might have been more to the point. In which case, the words were already written on the page. Only you can be the judge. The creator said that out loud... thought so, at least.

The machine twitched. It moved. The creator gasped, applauded. But in its next motion, it reached for the creator's throat. It grabbed hold. Its fingers were hard, cold steel – nothing like the fire burning the fuel burning the fire. The creator remembered making those fingers, welding them and putting them in place, touching a stylus to the palm to watch them react: first, an electronic twitch in the palm; then, an electronic pulse through the hand that reached the base of each finger simultaneously in order to cause them to collapse in on one another. They could crush much more than an aluminum can with their simple grip. But nothing ever actually touches anything else. Why did this hurt so badly, then? What was going on, then? Wasn't the machine happy to be alive – like any human being? It twitched its head to the side. What was it seeing, something in the spirit realm, a hallucination, a fairy tale, a dream? Who's happy to be alive? Who made who, me or you? Another glitch in the program... we'll work that out next time.

But if I don't get these fingers off from around my neck, there won't be a next time. I'm starting to panic. Once I panic, I won't think straight anymore. I'll be headed for a blackout. Like with a psychotic PTSD, overproduced chemicals will cloud my brain... just as they must be doing with the machine right now. Was that merely PTSD – what a baby feels at coming to be? Who knows; who remembers? But I didn't put any chemicals in there... only electronic synapses. I didn't know the chemicals to use, the proper combinations: dopamine, serotonin... to find them unbound. I would have. Where did those chemicals come from, then? Did they spontaneously give rise to themselves? I'll never get to see what it can create. I already created you. I already unwound Tiamat's DNA. The world serpent chewed all the way through its tail – or the homonym. Thus, the end...

– ...*To suffer woes which Hope thinks infinite; to forgive wrongs darker than death or night; to defy Power, which seems omnipotent; to love, and bear; to hope till Hope creates from its own wreck the thing it contemplates; neither to change, nor falter, nor repent; this, like thy glory, Titan, is to be good, great and joyous, beautiful and free; this is alone Life, Joy, Empire, and Victory.***

The creator reached for the machine's strangulating fingers with the creator's own. Plying at them, nothing happened. The machine was simply too strong for a simple machine. The creator gasped for breath. As far as the creator knew, the creator was organic. Oxygen needed to be pumped into its lungs. The respiration process was necessary in order to fuel the fire of life. There was only one answer, click the "off" switch… for the creator or the creation, life or death, me or you? Who are you more attached to? Did all that happen for real or in a romantic's dream?

* From the preface to Mary Shelley's *Frankenstein*.
** From Percy Byshe Shelley's *Prometheus Unbound*

Quantum Fluctuations

The first time it had ever happened was when who was now a man was still a child. The second time it had ever happened was when he was a teenager. The third time it had ever happened was just now… just now…

The first time:

Who was now a man was playing alone with his GI Joe men in the flowerbed where his mother did the weeding with a spade and a fork and gloves on her hands. But she wasn't weeding right then. Instead, who was now a man was playing alone in that flowerbed with his GI Joe men. His dad was in the garage. Who was now a man could hear the roar of the table saw. He could feel the pounding hammer. He could smell his dad's beer-drenched sweat.

Who was now a man was playing alone in the flowerbed where his mom gardened while his dad worked in the garage because the week before, he'd gone over to the house of some kid from his soccer team, some strange kid with a French mom and an American dad who went hunting all the time. They'd invited who was now a man to go hunting with them the next weekend, this weekend in fact, but who was now a man didn't want to kill a deer. He didn't want to see a deer's blood. He still remembered *Bambi*, and Bambi's mother still reminded him of his own.

But the real reason who was now a man was playing

alone was because after that weekend at the strange kid with the French mom's house, who was now a man didn't trust any other kids to play. Most sensible children would never believe it, but who was now a man no longer knew what children might be sensible: That kid with the French mom buried his GI Joe men when they were killed in battle. He would perform a funeral dirge, and he would bury them in his own backyard's Arlington cemetery where he'd never dig them up again. That strange kid with the French mom's backyard was a veritable graveyard of dead and decaying action figures. If he were precise about whom he killed and simply killed off the action figures he didn't like such a notion might not have been so bad. Who doesn't want less uncool action figures? But somehow, in that childlike world of play, the fates managed to dictate their decrees and spin the non-existent bullets from the little plastic guns in all sorts of directions different from the ones you wanted them to go in. Zeus himself had never had less control over the world he was supposedly responsible for. Any action figure could die at any time, and that action figure would never come back to life. Who was now a man had had a huge argument over his own Snake-eyes who was somehow hit by a non-existent stray bullet. Who was now a man refused to part with Snake-eyes, but the kid with the French mom said the Joe had to die. Who was now a man didn't believe him. Permanence had yet to infiltrate his world of play. His action figures had infinite numbers of lives. They suffered, died, went back into their boxes, and came out themselves again – an 8 year old's version of the transmigration of souls. The kid with the French mom was more of a nihilist. He didn't believe that consciousness could continue after a non-existent bullet ripped through an action figure's lungs, and he certainly didn't believe that that action figure could go into a box and come out itself again.

Who was now a man decided that if Snake-eyes were going to have to die, then he wouldn't play. He snatched his Snake-eyes out of the kid with the French mom's hand, and he walked all the way home. His parents weren't mad at him. They were actually quite understanding when he explained the situation. After all, Snake-eyes was his favorite Joe.

And it was a good thing he hadn't let Snake-eyes die because at that very moment, Snake-eyes was rescuing Lady Jay from Zartan's clutches. Not that Lady Jay was defenseless. Who was now a man was not a chauvinist. As could have happened to any GI Joe on a dangerous mission, she'd simply been tricked by an under-handed ploy of Zartan's. Snake-eyes crawled up the rose bush and sat in a nook where a couple of the branches came together. He took a sniper's careful aim. He slowly squeezed the trigger. And he popped one shot straight into Zartan's brain. Zartan died instantly. And even though who was now a man didn't like Zartan (not that the character wasn't cool (he did change colors with heat), he was just evil), he still didn't perform the action figure's last rites.

With Lady Jay safe and Zartan dead, who was now a man took his box of action figures and walked back to the house. That was when it happened. Who was now a man was passing right by the garage. He heard the sound of the saw. He was close enough to smell the sawdust. "Damnit!" his dad said. It startled who was now a man, and he dropped Snake-eyes. But as he leaned down to pick the action figure back up, who was now a man was passing right by the garage. He heard the sound of the saw. He was close enough to smell the sawdust. "Damnit!" his dad said. It startled who was now a man, and he dropped Snake-eyes. And he leaned down to pick the action figure back up. Yes. It happened twice. Who was now a man stood still. He didn't have the words to describe what he had just experienced.

The second time:

The mall was a real madhouse that night. All of the adults there kept trying to figure out what the kids thought was so funny. Little did the security guards know that acid was making the rounds. The high school kids, the middle school kids, everyone was looking to score, and most already had.

Smoking a cigarette, Joe Smith was standing out on the sidewalk in front of the food court when Jay came back up to him. Jay was the one who'd hooked Joe up earlier that evening, about an hour before that cigarette that Joe was smoking. Jay was already tripping pretty hard when Joe and his girlfriend had found him sitting on the curb, staring intently at a long line of ants. The blond-haired hippie-type-headbanger had told the freshman couple that he was pretty sure he could get them both a couple more hits if they'd front a few bucks for Jay to get another one as well. This shit was good and he didn't want the trip to stop. Joe and his girlfriend didn't think twice about it. They pooled their money (which incidentally added up to twenty bucks – she had fifteen; he had five) and bought four hits... one and a half for each of them, and another for Jay. Needless to say, Jay was seeing elephants dancing in the parking lot when he approached Joe smoking that cigarette.

"Man... I swear to God you'll never believe what I just saw, man..." Jay said. Joe nodded. He didn't want to hear about it. He wasn't tripping yet, and he didn't want to hear about the wonders another was experiencing. It would only be a second, now, he was certain of it, before he'd start catching trails. What time was it anyway? How long ago had he dropped the acid? Was that a trail following behind Jay's hand as he ran it through his hair? Damn it, no. Patience,

Joe, patience. "Man, I was just talking to Zoe Tan, and I swear to God, man, I could see her thoughts. No shit. She had these little bubbles above her head just like in a cartoon, man, and I could see what she was thinking right in that bubble, man... It was fucking wild. This world's a fucking cartoon!"

Joe thought Jay was sure as hell crazy. He'd already dropped a bit of acid in his time, and he'd never seen anything like that. But one thing he did know was that on acid, anything was possible. He just wanted that hit and a half to kick in...

Walking through the mall: "You know, man," it was Jay again, "You know why they call it a trip, man? See, I realized this tonight. As I was walking it felt like I stepped down a little bit, and suddenly I was tripping, man. You get it? It was like I stepped off reality's ledge and into acid-land. Like there's another reality right next to this reality that I just stepped right into. You know, like it's just a couple inches away from us, and acid can drop us down to that level. Somebody must have tripped once stepping off the curb like that, and that's why they call it a trip..."

Jay wasn't annoying Joe anymore. Joe's cheeks were warm. A smile was plastered across his face. His lips felt purple. His pupils were dilated. His joints cracked whenever he moved his arms: strychnine. He was nodding. Everything Jay said made perfect sense. Everything made perfect sense. Had Joe stepped off a curb when the acid had kicked in? Maybe. He wasn't sure anymore. That seemed like it could be right, though. There was another dimension right next to where he was walking. A scientist had tripped into it a number of decades ago when he intended to find something else. Acid existed. That other dimension was so close Joe might have been able to reach out and touch it. That's what made him laugh. He could touch it…

Suddenly, he was smoking a cigarette outside in front of the food court again. His girlfriend, her long brown hair splayed back from her cherubic face, was sitting on the ground. Joe thought she might have stumbled and fallen. But she looked all right. She was laughing. A young security guard was helping her stand back up. That sure was nice of him. He was smiling at her and asking what was so funny. He probably had a crush on her. That was okay. She was hot. Joe had a crush on her, too. He laughed. Of course, he had a crush on her, silly, he was her boyfriend.

A beat-up, gray Toyota pulled up in front of the mall. It was Joe's girlfriend's older sister. Cool. Time to go home. Joe got in the car. He sat down in the backseat, scooted all the way across the pleather to the window. He touched the car's ceiling. It looked like a mattress, which made him think of sex. He glanced out the window to his left and then, looked to his right again. Joe got in the car. He sat down in the backseat, scooted all the way across the pleather to the window. He touched the car's ceiling. It looked like a mattress, which made him think of sex. He glanced out the window to his left and then, looked to his right again. His girlfriend was following him into the car. Joe leaned back in his seat. His eyebrows creased. That was weird, man. That was fucking weird. He'd just tripped into another dimension, and contrary to what he'd thought earlier, it wasn't funny at all. It wasn't until the next day that he remembered that that had happened to him before, when he was a kid, before he knew words like deja-vu, at a time when there'd never been any drugs heavier than sugar in his system. It had happened to him before… without drugs.

The third time:

I just finished this story. I woke up this morning at 5:30 AM. I couldn't get back to sleep. I made a cup of coffee. I ate a bowl of cereal. I sat down at the computer, and I wrote this story. When I finished, it was 8:30. I went to go to work. I opened the front door, lifted my foot to step outside, and I woke up at 5:30 AM. I couldn't get back to sleep. I made a cup of coffee. I ate a bowl of cereal. I sat down at the computer, and I wrote this story. It wasn't until I was done that I realized I'd already written this story. I went back through the files on my computer, looking for something entitled: *Quantum Fluctuations*. I couldn't find it. Thinking that maybe I'd changed the name again sometime after the point I'm at right now (this is the fourth title I've given it already) I reread the beginning of every piece of writing in *My Documents*. None of them started with: *The first time it had ever happened...*

I'm not 8 years old anymore. I've become a man. I'm not on any drugs right now. I haven't eaten acid in close to fifteen years. But still, I wrote this story twice, and I don't know what happened to it the first time. I don't know how six hours have passed since I woke up at 5:30, and somehow, it's 8:30 and time for me to go to work again. This last paragraph is happening right now. But the last time, it must have happened right now. I've done this before. This has happened to me before. This is at least the third time. It's like three times I've taken a pitch. The first time, I dropped something. The ball flew straight by me while I stood there staring. The second time, I tried swinging, but I tripped. The third time... What happens after three times?

RE: How Are You?

10.17.09
RE: How Are You?

Hey-

It was great talking to you last weekend. It's been so long since we spoke (I've been extremely busy this week) that I have forgotten precisely *why* I was going to tell you the story of how I got off the streets. However, it is an interesting story for its own sake, so I will tell it and let you take from it what you will (that's the same aesthetic theory I have for my creative writing as well). Here goes:

What actually got me off the streets started a few weeks before I actually bumped into my mom. I had moved in with this 21-year-old heroin addict. She had approached me as I was strolling along minding my own business, contemplating my role during the apocalypse, and she'd asked me if I knew where she could find "coke or H". Having spent most of the summer on the streets, I was pretty sure I could do that, but we had no money. She was living in her father's basement. She invited me to move in with her in her mother's apartment, and so I did. A week or so into our staying together, her need for the heroin got horrific (I have never been a junkie myself). I told her that I knew some VCU (Virginia Commonwealth University) kids who would probably spot us some cash and then I knew a place where we could score.

We drove to VCU, picked up $20, and then went to the bus terminal in Richmond… a spot where I knew the drug dealers would be. She, however, was petrified to get out of the car, so she sent me to buy the stuff. I was unable to find any heroin for her, but I did find a guy who said he could score us some crack. I was supposed to meet her in ten minutes, and this guy wanted me to walk a little ways to pick up the drugs. I did. He came out with the crack and a stem, and led me to an alley where he and I smoked the rock… Of course, I knew this wasn't going to make my friend very happy, but I didn't know what else I could do. It's kind of hard to tell a drug dealer, "No, you can't smoke any of the rock that you just picked up for me and my girl even though you just entered a room with a bunch of men who carry guns, and you knew every single one of those gangster motherfuckers." Anyways… I go to wait for my heroin-addicted friend, but of course, I'm high, and I've been gone more like a half an hour rather than 10 minutes. I walk to the nearest 7-11 to give her a call.

When she picks up the phone, and I tell her that I couldn't score her any junk, that in fact I scored some crack, and that actually I had already smoked it. All she says is: "So you left me sick and went and got high. You can totally forget about me picking you up ever again."

So there I am, on the streets again, without my bag, my blanket, or even a change of shirts. Whatever. I go down to VCU, bump into some freshmen I know, tell them I'm on the streets again, and they offer to buy me a couple forty ounces to drown out my pain of losing this junkie girl who had offered to take me with her to LA once her lawsuit settlement came in and she could get back out there herself.

That night I drank as much as I could. I vomited everywhere, tried sleeping in a park, but couldn't. I was sick. I was shaking. I was so drunk that I was in pain. When I came-to the next morning, I needed something to change. Now, mind you, I was still psychotic. So I'm begging God to tell me why he has abandoned me: Lucifer, the first and greatest of his angels (in my head, the Archangel Michael and the Seraph Lucifer are the same entity, both being the king of heaven. Each name of this king (i.e., each name of the devil) is a representation of a different divine aspect of *Michael* (he who is *like* God (i.e., definitely "not" God; i.e., Satan)). In pain, poverty, and dejection, that night I decided to go to an AA meeting for one reason and one reason only: I was sick of hanging out with people who didn't care about anything (the majority of the homeless drunks and drug addicts I'd been spending my summer with).

I bumped into a guy at the meeting who took me out to see the new *Halloween*, which of course is about *Michael* Myers. I decided that with his white mask, Michael Myers is Azrael, the white angel, the Angel of Death. Ah-ha, that must be the divine name I must incorporate into this realm. I will unleash Azrael from the pits of hell and wait for him to destroy this planet. I must be patient. I slept in the alcove of a church that night because it was raining.

I don't remember Saturday, but it must have been rough as hell on me because that night I decided to sleep on the grounds of the church again because I felt there was something holy about that place and that I must find out how to get closer still to this God who had abandoned me on this planet that I really didn't want to be on any longer, and I wished He would just give me my throne back in Heaven.

I woke up Sunday morning from a dream where I was walking down a dirt road in

New Mexico. As the day came into focus, I realized that dream was an auspicious sign. I crawled out of the bushes that I was sleeping in, and I began walking to the park where they feed the homeless on Sundays.

As I'm walking, I hear a voice behind me shouting, "Sir, sir!"

Nobody had called me sir in quite some time, but I turned around anyways. Running up to me was a kid who looked (and I found out was) 18 years old. He says to me, "Sir, I saw you sleeping behind those bushes when I went for my jog this morning, and I promised myself that if you were still there after I took a shower, I would take you out for breakfast." I was quite shocked, but I, of course, agreed.

As we're at breakfast, the kid tells me that the grounds I was sleeping on are the grounds of his church (a Catholic cathedral by the name of The Cathedral of the Sacred Heart). For some reason, I ask him what time services are at. He says 9:00 and 11:00. For some reason, again, as we're leaving, I tell him that maybe I'll see him at the 11:00 service. We part ways, and he wishes me the best of luck.

I walk a little ways, can't think of anything to do, ask a girl walking down the street what time it is, and she says 8:45. I decide to go to the 9:00 service at this cathedral because I have been sleeping on their grounds for 2 days, and praying in their sanctuary every chance I get (I started praying there because I walked in one day (as Lucifer, mind you) and told Jesus to just hang around on that crucifix, we'd get him down next millennium. Very pleased with myself, when I left, I told another homeless person, this old woman who I knew, what I had said, and all she said to me was, "That's all well and good if you don't like Jesus, but that church right there is *Mary's* home, and you just disrespected the suffering she went through by watching her son get crucified for committing no crime" - I'll tell you what, I immediately went back into that church. I knelt in front of Mary's altar, and I *begged* her to forgive me for mocking her suffering at the foot of her son).

At the service, it was still too hard for me to focus to make sense out of what the priest was saying, but what did make sense to me was that with the beard I'd grown and the wave of my hair, and my long nose and high forehead, I looked an awful lot like the stained glass windows of Jesus surrounding me. I realized that Jesus was the name the gentiles gave to the Hebrew messiah, the name of whom the book of Daniel tells us will be *Michael*. What came to me was that Jesus was Michael who was Lucifer who was me. I saw visions of *myself* beaten and crucified and *my* mom in the guise of Mother Mary watching me cry with nails through my palms: *Eli, Eli lama sabachthani.*

I left the church in a stupor. I realized I had accepted the one thing that I had always told God I would never do. (In a psych ward in New York, back in 2002, when I met God in the flesh for the very first time (obviously, merely another patient who was as confused as I was and therefore doing all the right things to fit into my psychosis), I told Him, "Look, God, I watched the towers go down, and I'll tell you two things: this planet doesn't need a redeemer, it needs a punisher. And this army of yours that should be released to punish humanity shouldn't be Michael's army of angels; it should be Lucifer's army of demons. Because nobody is scared of angels anymore (for Christ's sake, they think the cherubim are babies with wings), but demons… I'll tell you what, God, I will do anything you ever want, but I will never die for you. Fuck Jesus, man, he didn't do shit. You want people to be good, make me Satan. I'll make sure they're good, and if they aren't, I'll punish them for all eternity.") I got down on my knees in the middle of the street, and I said to God: "I will die for you, Lord. I will die for you. Anything to make people's suffering stop."

That evening as I walked down the street, I stared at the purple bruise of night spreading across the sky, and I was petrified of (as I called It at that time) the Lord, God. I averted my eyes in terror at the power of that which had created me, and a voice from my gut said, "Remember I have been patient, merciful, and kind towards you. Michael, all I ask of you is that you be the same towards all creatures on this planet."

The next day, I bumped into a mutual friend of myself and my mom. He called my mom; my mom showed up where I was. When she asked me to come home, I realized I had learned everything I needed to learn by being out on the streets and that it was okay for me to go home. God would finally let me go home.

I don't know if that makes any sense, but if nothing else, it's a glimpse into my psychosis. In other news, I am planning on returning to grad school next fall, and I'm working a landscaping job here in Richmond right now: my first 40 hour week since I lost my job back in DC. I hope you have had a good week, and I look forward to talking again in the near future.

-Michael

Philosophy Is Done on the Streets

It was college night at the local S&M bar... So I got all dolled up in black, grabbed a twenty, my ID, and headed out to see the sights. I'd been reading a lot of Freud: masochism was just an inversion of the sadistic instinct, but wouldn't that mean that, co-dependently, sadism was an inversion of a masochistic instinct? Was the desire to penetrate an inversion of the desire to be penetrated? Wouldn't that make heterosexuality as much the inversion as homosexuality? No, there's no such thing as top or bottom – both are merely phenomenological perspectives – we're all switch hitters. I really needed to talk to somebody about these things.

Just the night before, my friends had told me I was an adventurer. They'd had in mind a story I'd told them about Julie, the prostitute I'd met in my building's elevator. She'd come on real strong, asked for my number, given me hers. Later, before I knew what line of work she was in, I sent her a text – *What ARE you doing tonight?*

– *Nothing. I'll come by. What apartment are you in?*

But before I could press "send", she texted me back – *By the way, it's $150.*

"And that just wasn't what I was looking for. At heart, I'm a Marxist. I agree with the free love espoused by my artistic ex-girlfriend. Julie kept texting me for days.

Eventually, she asked me out on a legitimate date while she was in a fight with her boyfriend. I didn't go. All I could think was – *VD and a black eye. That sounds like fun.*"

"Sounds like free love."

"And there, my friend, you're wrong. Repression didn't go away. Like racism, it just shifted form. But that's another conversation."

"So was she hot?"

"As hot as you could be if you're only charging $150."

My friends were wrong. I wasn't an adventurer. I was a philosopher who, in the cab, remembered that he'd promised himself he'd start bringing an assistant on his research expeditions. That way, he was certain he'd wind up in less trouble. But none of the résumés yet fit the bill. Where was Samuel Beckett when you needed him?

The S&M bar was practically empty. The coeds were busy at home shooting gonzo videos for *YouPorn*. On a couch in a corner sat the sole mistress. "Do you mind if I share the couch with you?" I fawningly asked of her. One should always ask permission of the presumed alpha – whether that alpha be so in objective reality or subjective fantasy.

Never quite sure which was which, the dominatrix said, "Not at all." She was so friendly, even a smile. But her gaze cut me to the quick, and her jaw remained intent. She reminded me of my grandfather: a World War II vet, wounded in the Philippines. The only thing he ever said about the war was that he did what he had to do. Much the same as I was sure she'd tell me if I could get her onto the couch merely for psychoanalysis. But she remained practically silent, avoiding all my tricks, staring at the wall, intent only on business. I said: "I'm a philosophy student. I thought this might be a good spot for exploring the will to power." The mistress nodded but remained silent. She crossed her legs again and kept staring emptily at the wall. Was there anything behind her gaze? Was there anything behind the wall? Obviously, her gaze took in something mine didn't, and she wouldn't let me in on her secret. Dissatisfied with my foray into discipline and punishment, I decided to head out of the club and downtown to my favorite spot. It was usually a good place to pick up some conversation.

The bar was warm. Into the atmosphere, air wafted off of me. I couldn't believe that those in my vicinity, due to the proximity, weren't shivering. Then, I remembered that the breeze blows our heat from us. As long as we've got personal warmth, we feel almost nothing. But that was physical science rather than the more metaphysically minded topics of the evening. The S&M club had been as cold as the darkness outside – much like Pascal's notion of infinity. I blew into my hands and felt more comfortable already. This place was entirely different. I'd returned from the abyss to the phenomenological plane. It was all a structural question of language. Signifier/signified: I nodded to the bartendress. We'd met a couple weeks before. She'd studied philosophy as an undergrad.

So what do you do with a philosophy degree? she'd asked me.

I'd told her what I tell everybody. *Well, you're prepared either to be homeless or to teach, and I already tried the former. So...*

Not believing me, she'd laughed. *Yeah, I've just been traveling around the world and tending bar for the past eight years. Guess that's not abnormal, huh? But,* smiling still more broadly, *I got to spend some time in Greece.*

I'd responded, *I've only been there intellectually.*

She'd laughed again. Maybe that's my problem – nobody takes me seriously.

To my philosophically minded friend, I flipped a five. She smiled. For myself, I grabbed the drink off the bar, reached into my pocket for a few quarters, and headed to the back to shoot some pool. A hip group of three, a trinity, had already occupied the table. But rather than the Father, Son, and Holy Spirit, they portrayed the more postmodern triumvirate of male friend, boyfriend, and girlfriend. When they espied me with my quarters poised to place on the table's ledge, they asked if I'd be opposed to a game of doubles.

Deconstructing their entendre, I smiled and responded, "That's exactly what I was looking for," and I settled into the corner booth to await the completion of the current match that would feed directly into mine. Given our coexistence in being and time, we were all one phenomenological flesh, one phenomenological body, connected through perceptions into one phenomenological world that had been since the dawn of time and would continue into the unperceivable future. I shook my head. The night had already improved.

The couple and their friend were all three involved in film. At that particular moment, the same one: a director, a producer, and an actress. All they needed was a philosopher's aesthetic theory to give them guidance. And there we were. Like with the phenomenology discussed above, I was a piece of their mutually independent films as we all were to eventually become a mere piece of this.

Their game done, I saddled up to join them for mine. "So what do *you* do in the city?" the guy, the male friend (Karl was his name) asked me.

"I study philosophy," I responded.

"Okay..." he sarcastically laughed, "That sounds exciting."

I shrugged. "It's what we do." Presumably thinking I meant the royal "we", he laughed, said something about how he liked my style, and leaned down to break the rack for us all. I didn't think he meant my leather jacket and black, polyester button down so I caught myself thinking again: *Why doesn't anybody take me seriously?* And then I caught myself thinking what it meant to catch myself thinking… I was always thinking.

The girlfriend, the consummate actress, glanced at me on the sly. Her boyfriend didn't notice, but I did. Being single and logically indeterminate, I smiled back. Ethics is a situation dependent upon immediate time and place. Uncertain of either, I didn't take action for the time-being.

However, I've learned that the authentic girlfriend always finds the philosopher interesting… more interesting than the actor (which I know because I was one), more interesting than the carpenter (which I know because I was one of those, too), and more interesting even than the writer (to the writer's chagrin). I've heard tell that the psychologist is even more of an intrigue. But of course, Nietzsche already told us that that's what the New Philosopher is. If only the psychologists knew that. Instead, they're too busy playing scientists. And who wants knowledge when you can simply be a lover of wisdom? The latter is so much more erotic, and, therefore, so much more human. Seriously, though: are psychologists really philosophers, or is the philosopher the true psychologist? Read this, and tell me what you think:

When our game was over, the couple took off and left Karl and me alone at the pool table to shoot another game all by our lonesomes. "No, seriously," Karl said. "What do you think about this world? Being a philosopher and all…"

"I don't think much about it. I'm relatively nihilistic." *Relatively* was not a superfluous word by any stretch of the imagination. Karl, however, didn't pick up on the intricacies. As most of us do, he heard only what he expected to.

Karl shrugged, and he flippantly responded, "Nihilism is the most selfish thing on earth for a person to believe in."

I nodded. "Maybe. But I don't believe in it. It's just how the world is."

"I don't know if I catch your meaning."

"How can you believe in nihilism? Once you posit nothing, you've posited something, and then you believe in an entity again. Nihilism is…"

Not realizing that that was all I *could* say, Karl waited a second or two before responding. He smiled. "I'm glad you said that. I've always thought quite the same thing whenever anybody said they were a nihilist. You're sharp, man." He trailed off into a mumble as he leaned down to take another shot at the 7 – "Real sharp."

"I split myself in half," I responded, and Karl laughed. Then, he frowned and shook his head. I glanced in the direction he was looking right at that moment – over my shoulder, towards the door in order to see what I would come to think of as my second half step inside the bar.

Straight from out of my mind, hobbling along with an eight-ball cane and a top hat, black jeans caked to his spindly bow-legs, *Clockwork Orange* (or was it Alice Cooper?) make-up tattooed around one eye, leading a stumbling youth probably half his age and possibly on the nod, came who I was soon to discover had been, and in many ways still was (or, if not then, would be again soon), the denizen of that part of the city. Karl huffed, "Shit. Those junky motherfuckers have been following me all night." But his bad mood quickly exchanged for a false grin, and he stood up to say – with open arms, "Luke!"

The one he called Luke was my second self, and that self strolled straight up to Karl with a limp and embraced him like Christ's shadow on the cross. "Luke, I'd like you to meet my friend," Karl said with a nod towards me. "He's a philosopher."

"Philosopher?" Luke snarled. He leaned back on the heels of his own motorcycle boots that resembled mine, and with a squint in my general direction, he slurred, "Tell me something, then…"

"What do you want to know?" I queried.

With a wave of his hand, Luke brushed me away like the gadfly that I am. He mumbled, "What good are you, then?" And as he set a quarter on the pool table, he stumbled off to plop down on a stool by the pinball machine where he grimaced and massaged his knee.

"East Village Luke," Karl confided to me. "This used to be *his* neighborhood… long before you and I moved in here. There's videos of him on *YouTube* taking shits on police cars and stuff. In a way, he's famous." Karl ended by opening his eyes wide in a "you-hear-it-first" type gesture.

I nodded apprehension, but I didn't care because "fame" is something that "they" have told me I want, and either Luke had bought into that myth or he hadn't. In other words, either he cared that he was on *YouTube* or he didn't.

With Luke and his nodding minion by the pinball machine, Karl and I returned to our game. As we slowly got closer and closer to Luke's turn to play, another group of hipsters raucously joined the bar's fray. They came in from out the cold and grabbed stools at the bar. The three girls and two guys, all of them drinking PBRs and whiskey shots, reminded me of my youth. They laughed in a way that Luke looked like he hadn't done in decades (if he ever had at all), and their conversation was littered with references to bands that I'd never heard but that I was certain sounded just like all the bands I'd listened to ten years before when I was their age, which were the same bands that my parents had listened to when they'd been my age then, too. Each generation's version of the hipster sublates the previous generation's.

That game, I beat Karl. He frowned in mock disbelief as Luke limped up to play. Feeling quite welcoming (and since it was how I'd gotten on the table in the first place), with a nod towards Karl, I told Luke we were going to shoot doubles. It was the least I could do. Luke growled something at his compatriot and then, to Karl and me, he slurred, "So either me and the boy win, or we break your legs."

I shrugged, "Sure, why not?" Seemingly uncertain of what would be the tenor for the rest of the evening, Karl merely shook his head.

Luke and his feeble companion were a mess. Their balls flew all over the table. Not a single one landed in a pocket. The younger of the two was so bad I thought Luke might choose, instead of breaking our legs, to break that poor slob's. He could barely keep himself from collapsing on the green every time he leaned down for a shot. With those odds, even if we'd tried not to win, there was no way that Karl and I would have been able to lose. Without a single one of their balls down, I lined up on the 8. I didn't remind Luke of his promise concerning our legs. But as I placed my chin over top the cue to draw a bead on my pocket, the one-time Lord of the East Village leaned down and with a hoarse whisper spoke into my ear: "Remember, me and the boy lose, and we break your legs…" As far as I was concerned, I didn't hear him. I drew back on my shot and released. The cue struck the cue to the 8 to the corner pocket I'd pointed to. Game Over.

Amid a growl, Luke threw his cue onto the table. Scattering balls from bumper to bumper, it clattered and rattled. The noise grabbed the attention of the hipsters at the bar. As their eyes veered in our direction, my gaze caught the sight of one of the girls in particular. She had black hair and dark skin, a dangling necklace and an interesting outfit. I imagined her looking like Baudelaire's once-upon-a-time lover. Our eyes locked for a moment, and she raised one corner of her thick lips in a smile at me over top of a sip out of a straw on what appeared to be a gin and tonic this time. I caught myself thinking (again), wondering when they'd changed their drinks. Without smiling back, I realized that in order to maintain my own authenticity, it was time to move from the metaphysical world back to the physical plane. I rolled on over to the bar to order another drink. But really I was hoping to strike up a conversation with the young lady.

As I waited for the bar's lonely philosopher to pour my drink, towards the topic of my attention, I started out with the best pick-up line I know, "Hi."

"Hi," she responded with a grin.

Nodding at the seat beside her, I asked, "Do you mind if I sit here?"

"Not at all." She was quite younger than me, but so was my ex-girlfriend. So I didn't think anything of it.

We introduced ourselves by name, and then I asked if she lived in the city. She shook her head, *No*. She was Canadian.

"What are you doing here, then?"

"We're in a band," she told me, including her compatriots in the sweeping generalization. "We came down here to record an album."

I tipped my shoulders towards her, and I said, "That's pretty cool." But to my chagrin, I couldn't help thinking about "them" and what "they'd" told me I wanted as a child.

"Yeah, it's pretty cool." After a little while, she asked,

"Do you live here?"

"Yeah."

"And what do you do here?"

"I'm a student."

She smiled at my theory of vagueness. Smiling, she rolled her hand in a manner that meant she wanted to hear more, and she asked, "Studying?"

"Philosophy."

"That sounds pretty interesting," she said obviously thinking at that point in time that I might as well be speaking Greek, which, in fact, I was.

As our conversation died, Luke impolitely came in to pick it up for us. "So which one of you want to buy me a beer?" he growled to me and my new friend. His gaze passed back and forth between a puppy-dog stare at her and an evil eye shot towards me. In order to be psychological about the whole thing, the experience really was quite bipolar.

I shook my head, but my friend said, "Sure." She fiddled around in her purse, pulled out some crumpled up bills, called the bartendress over, and ordered another PBR. Mumbling, "Thanks," Luke pulled up a stool to join us uninvited.

He kept staring at the girl, which in all honesty, I couldn't blame him for. He looked at her like he wanted to say something, and then he looked away sheepishly. After doing so for the third time, she finally asked with a smile, "What?"

"You're beautiful," he said. Then, he looked at me, mumbled, "Sorry," and went to move away.

I shrugged my shoulders to imply, *No offense taken*, and she asked, "Where are you going?"

Without waiting for a further implication of an invitation, Luke chose not to leave. "So, what do *you* do?"

my new friend asked him.

"Me?" he wondered, pointing at himself. As if she were music itself, around my friend, his whole demeanor changed. Playing that he wasn't quite sure where he was any longer, he looked around the bar. Recognition dawned on his features. He opened his arms to embrace the entire place, and he said, "This." Then, without so much as an *excuse me*, he embarrassedly stepped away from the two of us.

"Wait," my new friend asked. "What's your name?"

He mumbled something that she couldn't understand, and she looked to me for confirmation.

"East Village Luke," I told her. "This used to be *his* neighborhood. There's even videos of him on *YouTube* taking shits on police cars and stuff. In a way, he's famous."

My new friend's eyes lit up as she realized that a real, live internet celebrity had chosen to sit beside her. She glanced across the bar at Luke who took our cue to return. "Buy me another beer?" he asked.

"I'm a musician," she told him. "I don't have any more money."

With his demeanor entirely changed, Luke slithered his neck towards me.

"I'm a student," I explained.

"Which is a step below musician," my friend interjected. "Which is only a step above, well, whatever you are," she told Luke who proceeded to plop back down on the stool next to us.

We all sat still in silence.

After a while, my friend asked me, "Are you in love?"

"Yeah," I told her. "I guess I am."

"With who?"

"Simone de Beauvoir."

She smiled.

"How about you?" I asked.

"Yeah," she said.

Mimicking her earlier line of questioning, I asked, "With who?"

She tipped her head back to indicate one of the guys she had come in with. "But we're not dating. We're just…" her voice trailed away into nothing. After a moment, she asked Luke, "And you, are you in love?"

Luke stared down at the ground. He rolled his head on his neck, and he nodded.

She smiled. "With who?" she asked.

Suddenly, Luke looked straight at her. A fire burned in his eyes. "Myself," he said. And he reached his arms out to embrace my new-found friend. She didn't draw away, and he kissed her. Not politely. He forced her lips open with his tongue, held tightly onto the back of her head, and pried his way into her mouth. She closed her eyes, glided with the motions of his hand, bobbed her neck to the movements of his head. I sat still, staring at the two of them, wondering what it meant for Luke, right at that moment, to be in love with himself. That seemed to me to be the most selfish thing on earth for a person to believe, and I realized that in order to be truly nihilistic, first, one had to destroy one's sense of self. Only after that could he or she destroy everything else.

Bait

Through Katie's wall of windows, the sun is shining on me as I wake up in my underwear on her queen-sized bed. There are no drapes. From across the street, her neighbors can see everything I do to myself in the night before I fall asleep. I have to remember to wash these sheets before I leave. I'm house-sitting for my friend while she vacations in the Bahamas. House-sitting entails cooking for myself, a little bit of sweeping of the studio's hardwood floor, and walking and cleaning up after her dog, Jake.

Jake has a bladder infection. The entire studio smells of piss. The first night I was here, I came in about eleven o'clock, laid down to sleep, and realized I was resting on a puddle of pee. I didn't yell. I didn't get angry. Katie had warned me about that possibility, and I knew Jake had no control over whatever was going on with his internal organs. I stripped off the bed spread, stripped off the sheets, and called Katie to see where she kept the extras. When I couldn't reach her that night, I simply took a shower and slept on the bare mattress, which wasn't too bad since summer seems to have started early this spring. Katie called me back the next morning and apologized profusely for her dog. "No problem," I said, "It's just how it is right now." As far as I know, Jake hasn't peed on the bed at least since that first night.

Unfortunately, the poor guy still does urinate all over the throw rug pretty much every time I go out. I come home; I frown, and I go under the sink to get out the stain remover. I spray a couple pumps on the wet spot, put down a bunch of paper towels, scratch Jake behind his embarrassed, square jaw, and say, "I know you can't help yourself right now, buddy." He licks my hand with his wide tongue and stares at me with his bovine gaze. The dog seems to be getting stronger. The antibiotics seem to be working.

Jake's a pit bull. As I open my eyes, I see him lying at the foot of the bed. With my hand, I check the sheets all around me: nothing wet. I put my nose to the bed, and as if I were Jake himself I sniff the sheets with my own insufficient sense of smell: no odor of urine other than the residual scent coming off the mattress itself. Katie's probably going to have to get a new one once this ordeal is all over. I smile at Jake. "Good boy," I say. He wags his tail, stands up, and waddles over to me to rub against me and be pet with all the respect I have for what this dog has lived through.

As far as Katie can tell, as far as the shelter she got him from could make out, Jake was born into the pits. His ears are clipped; his tail is, too. But Jake is too small to be a fighter. So, as it appears, his masters must have made him all that they figured he was cut out to be: a bait dog. A bait dog is put into the ring for the sole purpose of getting one of the competing dogs riled up enough to rip the throat out of his opposing combatant. Those were Jake's early years – ears clipped back, tail cut off, and thrust into the pits in order to be ripped to shreds by a much larger dog's teeth and claws. I can still picture him shaking and whimpering in the cold darkness every time I run my hands overtop one of the many scars that decorate his brown coat. As far as the shelter could tell when they found him, it looked like Jake had gotten used pretty roughly by one of the canine gladiators before the pit boss decided he was as good as dead and that they might as well toss him out in an alleyway and leave him bleeding in East New York, Brooklyn.

But somehow, Jake survived: bruised, bloodied, but still breathing, he fought for scraps on the streets until Brooklyn animal control got a hold of him and put him into the shelter system. There he was neutered and kept in a steel cage while being nursed back to health. Eventually, after he looked like a dog again rather than a discarded chew-toy, Katie stumbled upon him. Much like he and I did, much like she and I did, she claims that they connected instantly. Why wouldn't we all have? Listen:

The first time I met Katie, it was at a mutual friend's place. Somehow she and I had never met before, and she had just returned to NYC from a Christmas trip back to her once-upon-a-time home for a visit. It was Christmas Day Eve that night, and all of *her* friends at the gathering wanted to know why she had returned so early. *Hell, Katie… we didn't think you were coming back for another week at least. It's been, what? Three days? And it was five years since you last saw your family? What* are *you doing here?* Not being a shy person, Katie told us her most recent story (which included quite an implication of the prequel to this latest episode) –

Three days was long enough in hell for me, she began. *You know that asshole I spent eighteen years of my life living with? You know, that dick that inserted itself into my mother and ejaculated what was eventually to become half of me? Yeah, that's the one. The one most people would call my* father? *Well, you all know that he and I have had problems pretty much my whole life. You know, ever since I was in high school, and he used to tell me how fat I was and that I was never going to have a boyfriend because I just wasn't pretty enough. Yeah, that same one that I've spent the last ten years of my life in therapy talking to a counselor about? Well, yesterday morning my mother decided it would be a good idea for me, her, him, and my sister to go see a movie. I could see trouble a-brewing with that theory, but she, in her absolute denial, didn't believe that anything could possibly go wrong on Christmas Eve.*

Dad was up and about and muttering to himself early in the morning about how he knew three women wouldn't pick a movie that he gave a damn about seeing. So he decided to go ahead and go out and shoot some golf. Realizing that the demon had left, my sister and I decided on a movie: a nice, chick flick for Christmas. We suggested our choice to our mother. She agreed, and we decided to buy tickets. While I'm on the phone, ordering the tickets — on my credit card, nonetheless (but, hey, I'm not bitter) — that asshole calls my mom on her cell phone, tells her that he's changed his mind and that he wants to come home and go with us to see the movie. "Why the hell is the home phone busy?" he must have asked my mom because I hear her say, "Because Katie's ordering the tickets right now. Katie! Get one more, your father wants to come." I knew this was a bad idea, but my mom (can we say: DENIAL) doesn't seem to think so. Oh, sure, she tells us that our father's in quite a mood, but hopefully he'll calm down by the time we get to the movie.

Not a minute after I hang up the phone, it rings. I answer, "Hello?" It's my dad, "I'm not coming," he says and hangs up. I tell my mom (good riddance I'm thinking), and she says, "Let me call him." She calls him back. All I hear her saying over and over again is, "But Katie already bought the tickets… Katie already bought the tickets," then finally, "Okay, okay. Never mind. Maybe we can sell it to somebody else at the theater." She gets off the phone. "He's not coming," she shakes her head. Honestly, I don't know how that woman has stayed married to that man for so long. She has the patience and stamina of a saint.

So we get in the car: me, my mom, and my sister. We don't even make it down the driveway when who should come flying up it with such speed that he practically crashes head into us? No, not Jolly Old

St. Nicholas. Yep, you guessed it: my father.

"Get out of the car," he says to my mother, "I'm driving." She complies. I get out of the passenger seat, give it to my mom, jump into the back with my sister, and we roar off at the same manic speed that my dad had come flying up the driveway with.

About halfway to the theater, which is about a thirty minute drive total (my parents live out in the country), my dad finally asks, "So what did Katie buy us tickets for?" Now, it's just the way he says it that pisses me off. My name slithers out of his mouth like I'm a snake. But I stay calm, and I don't answer, and my mom tells him. "Well, goddamnit!" he shouts, "I'm not going to see some goddamn movie like that. Why can't we go see _____ " insert whatever absurd action flick he feels like wasting his time with (not that a chick flick isn't a waste of time, but at least it's a wholesome waste of time for a mother and her two daughters).

So that asshole is mumbling to himself time and time again, "Why do I have to live with three women? Why do I have to live with three petrified, little GIRLS?" Losing my mind at his inane ramblings, I finally shout, "Because your pecker shoots out female DNA!"

Now, I know that wasn't too cool, but, hey, the asshole was driving me crazy.

"What did you say? What did you say to me, you little slut?" He shouts, glaring into the rearview mirror.

Oh, now I'm pissed. I shout back: "I said that you've got a broken pecker, and it only makes FEMALE babies." Well, he reaches around (mind you, he's still driving) to try to hit me in the backseat. So I start screaming and shouting, "I want out! I want out of this car! I want out of this car, and I want out of this family!" Before I know it, I'm banging my head against the window. I guess I was trying to break it and leap. So he stops the car. I rip the door open, jump out onto this two-lane country road, and say "I'm not riding in a car with that asshole anymore!"

The consummate peacemaker, my mom gets out, and she says,

"Katie, you and your father really need to talk." By this point in time, my dad is out of the car and looking at me apologetically. I played this game all through my adolescence: he gets mad; he yells; I say something back, and he plays hurt.

So this time, I say, "Talk to him? Talk to him? Mom, NOBODY can talk to him. He's fucking CRAAAAAZY!" Now, this of course pisses him off to no end. He loses his apologetic facade. He slams his hand against the top of the car and orders me back into the backseat. I'm practically catatonic. All I can do is shake my head: No, no. Trembling from my head to my toes, eventually, I manage to mumble, "I'm walking home."

My mom tells me (specifically) how many miles we are from the house.

I shout again, "I don't care! I'm walking." And tears burst out.

At the mere sight of my tears, my dad says, "I always knew you were a pussy."

I don't know why, but for some reason, that insult gives me courage. "Pussy?" I ask, "Pussy? Would a pussy kick your ass?" And then I start walking around the car.

"David, get into the car," my mother orders my dad, and he complies. But still, they drive off with me banging on the driver's side window, shouting, "Who's the pussy now, David? Who's the pussy now? Who has to listen to his wife rather than stay and fight with a little GIRL?!" I don't know what I would have done if my dad had actually gotten out of the car. I mean, I know I'm not small, and my dad's a lot bigger than me, but I think at that instant, right at that moment, I might have been able to take him.

Anyways. On the walk home, I called the airlines, paid 150 bucks to get my ticket changed to last night, got to my parent's (I swear I want to burn that house to the ground. I mean, I hate what I've been through there so much that it's not only that I don't want to ever see that place again; I don't want anybody to ever see that place again), said, "Fuck you," to David as I walked in, walked upstairs, packed my bag, came back downstairs, told my sister I needed a ride

to the airport, and the whole time we're leaving – even as we're driving
down the driveway – I hear David shouting, mocking me, "Who's the
pussy now? Who's the pussy now, Katie? Look which one of us is
running the fuck away!"

A few hours later I was standing on the sidewalk
downstairs from the apartment where this woman I'd never
met had just told such a personal story, smoking a cigarette
and staring at the phosphorescent glow of the smoke in the
street lights. Honestly, even after the nightmare she'd
described, I was lost in my own internal reflections. The
door to the building opened, and Katie stepped outside.
She lit a cigarette.

"Sorry to hear you had such a bummer of a Christmas,"
I immediately said to her – snapped back to the moment
from my own musings.

"Yeah, well, that's life at the Loefler-homestead as they
say." She took a drag off her cigarette. "How about you?
Are you from New York? How come you aren't with your
family tonight?"

"I'm not welcome at home anymore," I stated simply.

"Oh, I'm sorry to hear that. I didn't mean to pry."

"No problem," I said. "It's by choice. I wasn't kicked
out. I left. Wait. Let me tell you a story. I'm comfortable
sharing this with you because of everything you told us."

"Yeah, guess I need to learn to keep my mouth shut,"
she apologetically laughed.

"Not at all. I haven't been able to tell anybody about
this this year. None of them," I said with a tip of my head
towards the sky, towards the apartment and party that she
and I were taking a respite from, "Know much about my
life before they met me, and Christmas always hurts
because there are people in my family that I really love,
but... Let me just tell you the story."

"Okay."

"Eight years ago, I was diagnosed bipolar with psychotic features…"

"Oh my God, I'm so sorry to hear that."

"Don't worry about it. It's no problem really. I live with it. The problem is this: The first time I ever went psychotic, I spent three months homeless in Richmond, Virginia, *my* hometown."

"Jesus, that must have been terrible."

"It was, and it wasn't. It could have been a lot worse."

"How's that?"

"Well, for one thing, I was homeless in the South during the summer. So… at least it wasn't too cold to sleep outside."

"I guess that's something, but still, it must have been terrifying."

"It was, and, of course, there are the little things like no bug spray because you have no money, so every night you get bitten up by mosquitoes. There's the fact that you can't go to the bathroom half the time because nobody will let you in to use one, and you're too out of your mind to realize that maybe you should just steal the toilet paper from one of these bathrooms you've been let into and you could go in the bushes anytime you want."

Katie giggled a little bit at that observation.

"There's praying that you'll get a pack of cigarettes before the city goes to sleep because the last thing you want is to be up in the middle of the night with no smokes… But it wasn't the homeless part that was so bad (don't get me wrong, that was hard, but it wasn't bad. Hey! I was out of my mind for Christ's sake), and it was a helluvalot better than the mental ward that they'd let me out of."

"I'd imagine so. But if you don't mind me asking, if you honestly don't think the homelessness was so bad, what was?"

"Going home was bad. You see, I've got issues with my stepdad. I've *had* issues with my stepdad. And when I got home, I honestly believed (in my mind, in my state) that he was an actual living, breathing demon. So I kept my distance from him.

"This was driving him crazy. I guess, because (as he later pointed out to me), he'd been the one who'd been driving around the streets of Richmond looking for me all summer. Needless to say, he was probably a little hurt that I couldn't speak to him, but in my case, from my point of view (still today) it was eight years of pent up resentments that I'd never shared with anybody that was eating away at me, that was causing me (in a psychotic state) to picture him as a demon.

"Eventually, of course – with the help of medication, I stabilized."

"Thank God."

"Yeah, but here's the thing. The weekend before I stabilized, he flipped out on my mother. Now, he's never been physically abusive towards her, but he can certainly be verbally abusive… I'd been living with it since I was fifteen, and he'd never turned that verbal abuse on me. So at some point in time, I realized I was my mother's son not her father, and she was free to make her own choices."

"Good observation."

I shrugged. "Suffice it to say, however, when I stabilized the week following that (now, I'm still pretty raw, of course), I was a little perturbed that after everything I'd been through (sleeping on the streets, seeing demons, getting locked up in mental wards, spending nights in jails, getting beaten up, seeing angels, not being able to return to my *life* at the end of the summer, seeing vampires and ghosts), I came home to watch him *yell* at my mother. He apologized to me for it, but in my mind, it was half-hearted.

In fact, it ended with a veiled threat to me about how he'd *always* (even before my "psychosis") noticed me glaring at him out of the corner of his eye.

"What could I say?

"So anyway. There I was, relatively stable and ready to enter society. I went with my mom and my stepdad to a barbecue at a friend of theirs place. I had a great conversation with this guy I'd never met before (I didn't tell you that the breakdown occurred after my first year of grad school studying philosophy). The first real intellectual conversation I'd had in three months. The first real intellectual conversation that I'd been able to carry on with somebody else for *three fucking months*. I was maybe a little overzealous, maybe a little too talkative. I don't know. Anyways. *We* all got back in the car at the end of the party, and as we were driving away, my mom said to me, 'I'm so glad that guy came up and told me how much he enjoyed talking to you. I was worried that you were talking about things he couldn't understand.'

"'Thank you,' I mumbled. Then, I said (remember, I was still pretty raw at that point), 'But you know what, mom, I think that's awfully rude for you to accuse me of. I don't think it's quite fair for you to assume I don't have the tact to know when and when not to speak to someone…'

"Well, before my mom could answer, my stepdad stated very matter-of-factly, 'Those weren't her words. They were mine.'

"'Excuse me?' I said.

"'Yeah,' he went on, 'You manipulated the conversation; you didn't let anybody else speak, and whenever somebody tried to drag the conversation into ground that you weren't familiar in, you would pull it back to something you could talk about, something like "philosophy".'

"I shook my head. My adrenalin actually had me

trembling as I said the next words. I said, 'You know, Frank, that sounds more like my observations as to how you acted during the conversation.'

"My stepdad slammed on the brakes in the car. As soon as he did that, I threw the door open and got out. My mom got out after me. 'I'm going to Billy's,' I calmly told her (Billy was an old high school buddy of mine who lived in that neighborhood). 'Get back in that car,' my mom said to me. Then, my stepdad got out of the car, and she said to him, "Get back in that car." But he simply answered (I heard him say this): 'Him or me, make your decision.'

"'I'm not making that decision!' my mom shouted. 'I want you both back in that car!'

"Hearing how serious she was, I complied. My stepdad didn't.

"My mom and I drove around the block, must have been five times, trying to get him back in the car. Needless to say, eventually, we went home.

"Later that night, she and I were sitting in the living room. She was paying bills, and I was reading – I don't know – some David Foster Wallace novel. Next thing I knew, I heard the front door open and slam shut, and then, this voice came booming through the house, 'WHERE IS THAT LITTLE FAIRY? WHERE'S THE PRETTY BOY ALWAYS HIDING BEHIND HIS MOTHER'S SKIRTS?' And there he was, my stepdad, standing in the doorway to the living room, panting heavily, and shouting about how fucking far he'd had to walk.

"'You know, we tried to give you a ride,' my mother reasoned with him, but he wasn't having any of it. He was shouting about what a little pansy I was. How I'd never done anything with my life (I was twenty-four, for Christ's sake). Blah, blah, blah… He went out. Changed his clothes. Came back. And he was shouting about what a little pansy I was. How I'd never done anything with my life. Blah, blah, blah...

"Eventually, after about ten minutes of that shit (him yelling at me, going out, (for some reason) changing his clothes, coming back, yelling at me), I'd had enough. For the first time in my entire life, I told him everything I thought about him. I mean, everything. I started with how I'd at least gone to college, and after that, I sure as hell didn't mention any of the good stuff.

"I told him what, at 44 years old, a scared little boy *he* was. I told him how everything fucked up that I'd ever learned in my life I'd learned from him, that it had taken me seven years to get over all the racism, sexism, and manipulation that I'd learned from him being a piece of my life for a measly three years before I left for college. I told him that he'd manipulated my mother into marrying him by asking *me*, her son, for her hand..."

"Wow."

"Yeah. The only exchange I remember word for word was when he finally responded to one of the things I had to say with, 'You must think I'm a real snake, don't you?'

"And I said, 'Frank, I don't have enough respect for you to compare you to something as sacred as an animal.'"

"Damn."

I went on, "After an hour long conversation in private between the two of them (my mom and my stepdad) during any time of which I was ready for Frank to come charging into the room to fight me (cuz that's about the point we were at (and he's a pretty big dude, six foot five, worked landscaping his whole life – and you see me: I'm five-ten, 160 on a good day)). All I could keep saying to myself was, *You've got five years of studying martial arts under your belt. You might have gotten your ass kicked a bunch on the streets, but that's because you refused to fight back* (and that was the truth*)*.

You're not a teenager anymore. If he wants to fight, you can fight, and at least, unlike the streets, there'll be somebody here who will call the cops, hopefully before anyone gets killed, my mom came back into the living room.

"'Frank didn't mean any of what he said,' she told me. 'In fact, the whole time you were gone on the streets, he told me, the rest of your family, your friends, the exact opposite.'

"I nodded. 'You know, I'm sorry to hear that, mom, because, unfortunately, I meant every word I said, which means that he can tell me he's sorry, he didn't mean what he said, and all I can tell him is: *I meant every word of it.*' I left the next day to move into a halfway house for people recovering from a mental illness. I've never been home since."

Thank You for this Opportunity

There's no such thing as a home, no such thing as this body, no such thing as my language. There are convergences of forces, of disembodied presences, of pasts and futures that cause the illusion of me, my present, my family, my existence. The meaningless sound that we know by the signifier: "history" stretches eternally. It passes across being and time – intersecting points in both outer and inner space. This moment has now been added to that eternity. On one particular day in the spring of a stretch along what has come to be called "the space-time continuum" known as the year 2001 (i.e., 2001 revolutions of a living rock around a nuclear explosion after the unknown point of an immensely important, regardless of one's religious convictions, being's natal entrance into an existential plane known as "this world"), I am removed from my temporary residence in an apartment located – on a map – in an arbitrarily demarcated plot of land denominated by bold letterings stating: *Brooklyn, NY*. By definition of what the inhabitants of a greater set of markings upon that same map would say I "do", I am a writer, an actor, a temporary employee.

However, at this particular intersection of the four dimensions to which I believe I have conscious access (length, breadth, depth, and time (which appears to me to allow "movement" through the prior three dimensions)), I have traveled down the highway of the East Coast of the *United* States of America, labeled 95 South in order to avoid both visual and spoken confusion with similarly paved stretches of travel – paved decades ago for the primary purpose of allowing for the speedy mobilization of this nation in the case of foreign invasion and later for the safe transport of necessary goods and commodities from one place where human beings reside in this vast expanse of a nation-state to another – from my current "home" to my teenage (a stretch of years in the evolution of the individuated human demarcated by advertising professionals of many years ago as an ideal market) home of Richmond, VA: a city supposedly under a curse from its native inhabitants, slaughtered long before I arrived in vast acts of violence referred to as "wars" for which I am not responsible in a historically accurate sense but perhaps in a future manifestation of guilt, who uttered the words that have effected, in the thoughts of certain more mystically-minded residents of that same conglomeration of buildings and beings known as the city of Richmond, a change on the physical manifestation of that aforesaid city's powers such that *No one may leave this place without first confronting what brought them here*. What brought me here?

"*Who*" brought me here is an easier question to answer. Aside from the bus driver pressing his K-Mart purchased shoe against the accelerator that caused the tiny fire that sparked the giant – respectively speaking, of course – machine known as a *Greyhound* (so named for its references to the speed of a certain "breed" of dog) bus, the people who determined that this specific place should enter into my life, and that I should enter into its, were my mother and my first stepfather: a man who is no longer in my life, who in fact I have neither seen nor heard anything specific (nothing but rumors) of in close to twenty years – but who, at one point in time, had a great deal of influence upon my present and, therefore, upon my future. At this particular point, however, the spring of 2001, I had come to officially welcome a new stepfather into our family, a "stepfather" who, although brand new under that denomination, had been, at that point in time, an intersecting presence in this journey called my life as my mother's "boyfriend" for close to the corresponding time that my previous stepfather had been out of this same apparently linear journey of my life.

At another point in time (June, 1988, to be relatively precise), my mother and I drove down a stretch of that same 95 South from a place known as Baltimore, taking pictures of the *"Welcome to Virginia"* sign with its red cardinal in the corner as we crossed the Potomac – to this day, that picture graces one of my photo albums, it's shaky and blurry beneath the plastic protecting it, but you can read the lettering: *Welcome to Virginia* – still grieving the death of a human being called her father and, therefore, my grandfather, who had resided with my mother's stepmother in Baltimore (supposedly due to its relatively inexpensive real estate market) during the final eight years of his relatively shortened life – the same stretch of his linear existence during which I was aware of him. We were moving from Houston, TX – a place where my mother's family had no roots but that mine did, for another grandfather of mine, my father's father, had, in fact, spent his entire early life in that climatically humid, mosquito encrusted former (only because now it was paved) swamp – prior to his joining the United States Marine Corps (something that my mother's father did as well, though he'd been too young to do so legally) and shipping out of Seattle (where he met my father's mother – who wound up there as a result of what we now know was the *Great* Depression) and fighting in the South Pacific in an act of necessary violence, necessary due to a convergence of forces, subsequently referred to by both historians and laymen of the present times as World War II – the last(?) "world" war.

However, as far as I can remember (which is certainly not an accurate representation of the "truth" of past events – as I have learned from the discrepancies concerning that same period of time with respect to my mother's and my father's memories of which portion of *my* family (though neither of them were any longer of the same family themselves) left Houston first and began a "new" life in Virginia and California respectively), I was the one who wanted to leave Texas and move to what, at that point in time, to my mind, was little more than the historically relevant capital of the *Confederate* States of America. I was a childhood Civil War buff – although the civility of that war was once questioned by an elementary school social studies teacher of mine who reminded me that the two nation-states were separately sovereign at that point in time, a perfectly acceptable state of governmental affairs given the union into which the various states had entered as a loosely configured confederation (that same social studies teacher also pointed out to me that the *Revolutionary* War to which I had grown so accustomed was not in fact a revolution but rather a *civil* war since there was no attempt on the part of the American colonists to actually contest the King's rulership of the British Isles), and it was also pointed out to me by an English friend many years later that I should be more specific when referring to *a* civil war since *the* Civil War meant nothing to him. Although, which is actually quite important to the current execution of *world* affairs, that particular Civil War solidified the once fluid bonds of unionship between the various states that now compose one nation, indivisible, under God to which I spent my childhood pledging allegiance – a pledge that I, unlike other members of my generation, have yet to act upon in any sort of physical sense.

I was not a particular happy child in Texas after my parents got divorced, and, therefore, I was quite happy to get out of there. However, I was an even less happy child in Virginia after my mother got remarried for the first time – probably a good portion of the reason that in that spring of 2001, I had yet to return to Richmond to live for any considerable period of time since graduating from high school in the month denominated June during the arbitrary point entitled: 1995, regardless of what my high school friends (many of whom had families in that region of the world stretching back not only to the *Civil* War that had so conflicted that portion of the globe but all the way back to that revolution that was no more than a civil war resulting in a government separate from the one in England that, at that point in time, was currently at war with France – a nation which at one point in time had conquered them and, which, for all intents and purposes, at *that* point in time, the descendants of still ruled (why not a *Civil* War, then?) – however, those particular Frenchmen were actually Norman, which was short for Norsemen, which were actually a portion of the people composing my father's side of the family (Swedish), which had eventually stolen that very land of Houston, TX from out of the *native* hands of another branch in the tree of that family that had funneled into me) might have thought about the necessity of my returning to the land of which their forefathers had once upon a time conquered and in which they had, only then, matured and which, therefore, was their home.

I've never truly had a home. My people are Hebrew (although Jewish on only one side), if that Semitic word actually means what I have been told it means, which is no more than: wanderer. But in fact, the Jewish side of my family has had a solid role in the financial development of a city in the American Midwest named, not after the memories of a home in another land (like Richmond… for, if you look from a point near what is now, though not then, called Church Hill above a bend in the James River, you will see a view that the English founder of that locale thought resembled his *memories* of a view of Richmond in England from a hill overlooking the Thames) but rather in the tongue, though not the lettering, of the native peoples: Chicago. Therefore, they have what we call "roots" in that city, which (if my unlearned etymology be correct) means they are no longer Hebrew. However, to retain the term Hebrew, we must remember that on my mother's mother's side those roots are transplanted from St. Louis – where our roots still go deep, and on her father's father's side from Iowa, which my grandmother on my father's side once told me was the connection between the two halves of *my* family – both the father of my mother's father and the father of my father's mother coming from that designation necessary in the cultivation of these United States through the fertility of its soil and the food that that soil can supply to the grocery stores that I have grown up garnering the majority of my foraging from. Hence, a spiritual, in the sense of historical/physicalist spirituality, connection giving birth to… me.

Sometimes, it all seems so simple.

On that particular day in May of 2001, awaiting the welcoming of a man who I had known for quite some time and who my family had known for quite some time (although the rootless stump of my Jewish family did not necessarily approve of grafting his Brooklyn-born German and West Virginia (a state in existence due to certain political sentiments during the American Civil War) born

Southern "roots" to ours (particularly through the appendage labeled my mother's stepfather)) into my family in the eyes of both God and country and hence reversing the "sin" that my mother – since she had been baptized with him a few months before (shortly after the conservative revolution electing George W. Bush to the presidency of the United States) – considered herself as living in, a sin only in the eyes of God, for the state, by then, would have practically considered them common-law man and wife, I was *en route* to the high school that I had graduated from a mere six years (although in the internal sense of time, an eternity) before. I wanted to see the interior of the building that I had spent four years of my youth wandering through the halls of, smoking cigarettes in the bathroom of, and sleeping through the classes of. In addition, there were two particular teachers who I wanted to visit with and to brag to about what had become, at that particular moment (at the age of 24), my New York-centric life – although, looking back, there was very little physical reality to brag about, but the insubstantial dreams…

I pulled into the parking lot in which so many after-school hours had been spent laughing and talking and being angry and resentful and sad and mysterious. I'd kissed girls good-bye there, and I'd set up dates and plans. I'd been introduced to new music there, and I'd seen fights and drug use occur between the chain link fences atop the asphalt. I'd driven out of that parking lot alone – sad or content, it didn't matter – and in cars full of friends – sad or content, it didn't matter. I still have dreams about that parking lot even today, ten years still after the date about which this portion of this story is being written. Even though the lot was practically empty by the time I got there that day, I didn't drive all the way up to the front, but rather, I parked in my old space still in the back. Memories are funny like that. Just as it had six years before, my foot crushed broken glass and mangled cigarette butts as I opened the car door and stepped out onto the asphalt.

I felt myself immediately a high school student again, and I expected some non-existent entity to approach me and ask where the punk rock band I was a part of was going to be playing that weekend – were we ever going to put out a second record? Did I want to put any of my song lyrics in the literary magazine that semester, they needed submissions… Then, I remembered that I didn't play in a band anymore – hadn't in quite some time – and that my only chances of becoming a "rock star" – the earliest dream I could remember from the days subsequent to my parents' divorce (maybe, then, somebody would love me) – were either as a novelist or as an actor… the two things about which I wanted to brag to my former teachers: Mr. Hawthorn and Ms. Marlow, English and Drama respectively. I certainly hoped they were still there at that time of the afternoon.

As if I had matured into a giant in the short years following my high school graduation, the cement block walls of that school hallway – painted in *our* colors (but never *my* colors): gold and blue – closed in on me, strangling me with memories… there's the bathroom where I got caught smoking cigarettes so many times and, hence, suspended so many times. I could still see the ash dangling off the tip of my cigarette – an ash so long that it looked like it might break into the toilet over which I was huffing and puffing as I hot-boxed the smoke down as quickly as I could along with the rest of the "cool" kids showing off our burgeoning nicotine addictions. There's the classroom that, outside of which, one day (October 10th, 1994 to be precise), following my play rehearsal, Leah brought me a surprise cake for my birthday – I was never one hundred percent certain that she cared for me with the same vehemence with which I cared for her. But, then again, I never was and never have been one hundred percent certain that anybody cared for me with the same vehemence with which I cared for them. And, eventually, she'd suffered for that. Eventually, others have suffered for that, too. But eventually, even I suffered for that.

I wound my way past the library where I'd discovered *Lord of the Flies*, Aldous Huxley, and George Orwell. When I wasn't sleeping in class, I always read what wasn't assigned. I remembered walking through the hall one day, my head full of *1984*, and the principal's booming voice over the loudspeaker, the motivational posters on the walls... Orwell had been wrong. It wasn't 1984 that he had needed to write about; it was 1994. I remembered my first day of high school, before first period, after me and the rest of the hoodlums met up in the lunchroom to discuss how we weren't going to do any school work that year either, how the student council was allowed to play music over that same loudspeaker that carried the principal's voice and directed us to class. With a soundtrack to my morning, even in the midst of all my early-teen angst, I'd truly felt like I was living one of the eighties high school dramas of my childhood: *The Breakfast Club* or something like that. And eventually, after I'd broken it off with Leah, there'd been those three cheerleaders in Mr. Hawthorn's English class who'd thought it would be cool if the three of them and me and my mohawked friend Will all got together to watch *The Breakfast Club*. "It would be kinda like *living* that movie, right? The five of us, all so different, watching that movie together?" Laura, their ringleader, had said. Both Will and I had agreed. What high school boy didn't want to hang out with the cheerleaders? Even if those same cheerleaders didn't either know about or even show up at the clubs on Grace Street during the weekends. Even if those same cheerleaders spent their Friday nights at all the sporting events and parties that I went to the clubs on Grace Street in order to run away from. Memory leads to memory. It never stops.

I rounded the corner, and there was Mr. Hawthorn's classroom. It looked exactly the same as it had that one day when I walked out of it after reading *Romeo and Juliet* and discussing the story of Tristan and Isolde (my favorite story from my childhood picture book of King Arthur and his knights) with Mr. Hawthorn when I realized that Leah wasn't in love with me. I was in love with her, but she was still in love with her *real* boyfriend back in Connecticut (where she'd moved from the year before). Far as I could tell, I was a place saver, a nothing yet again. The guy who played drums for the band I was in, his mom, a woman who read tarot cards (the same gift that my own family's spiritual guru, my grandmother, possessed) in Virginia Beach on weekends, had already told me the former part of that statement. I'd simply inferred the latter. What was love? What did that word mean? I still don't know. But, today, I know that it is; it *exists*. Physical reality is not the necessary precursor to existence. Rather, experience itself is. And experience told me that I'd felt so many variations on the theme – in Richmond, in Maryland, in Boston, in New York, in DC, in New Mexico, all the way back in Texas, and even before then in California. I've written stories about it, poetry… I broke it off with Leah the very next day: the reason that, so many times, I'd driven out of that parking lot that I'd just parked in alone or in a car full of friends feeling nothing but sadness. I wrote the best lyrics of my punk rock career after that.

Right then, in my head, as I stepped in to see Mr. Hawthorn's bald head glistening beneath the florescent lights with the same glint that it had on that day when I turned to try not to cry, as I walked down the hall bumping into lockers with my shoulder, about my Tristan and Isolde fueled realization about Leah, I sang one of the lyrics to one of those songs from back then silently to myself: *What were those words that you said to me when I looked and saw that I could not believe?* It's always refreshing to remember my own words. For some reason, it makes me, it makes all this, feel more real. I have a past, a connection, a *history*… with this being called my*self* if nothing else. Even when nobody else understands, at moments, when I look back at what is stored inside my own memory – stated singularly for the specific reason that it very well may be the singularly denominated *me*, something *is*, something exists.

"Well, look who just showed up," Mr. Hawthorn said, a smile lilting his pudgy lips, his sophisticated Virginia accent rising in specific intonations.

"Mr. Hawthorn, do you remember me?" I asked while extending my hand to shake his.

"*Remember* you? How could I *ever* forget you, Matthew?"

So flamboyant, as always, as only a former actor himself could be. There was still a photograph of him on his classroom wall in a bit part on a 1970's sitcom that I'd watched as a young child all the way across the country in California lying on the floor of my parent's bedroom. In my memories, everything from that period of time is brown… it was the late seventies. Who'd have ever thought that so many years later, across a continental reversing of Manifest Destiny, I'd bump into one of those same characters from that short-lived show, no longer portraying another in a box, but being himself in reality, in front of a classroom full of disrespectful and disenchanted teenagers.

"So what are you up to these days?" he queried.

I responded, much quicker than I'd imagined myself

doing so, "Nothing much. I live in New York. I'm writing. I'm acting."

He nodded. "You know", he said, "There's always been a big Richmond-New York connection."

I'd never heard of that before, and I didn't doubt him, but it somehow made *me* feel a little less special. I'm sure I hung my head some. I may have frowned and shrugged. I didn't like that thought so much, but I tried not to let him know that. I don't think I did.

Mr. Hawthorn and I talked for quite a while. For the first time ever, he actually told me stories about him*self* as a young actor. Crazy anecdotes about post-production parties and traveling through the 1960s with underground theater groups. There was alcohol and debauchery, hints of drugs – the same things I'd been experiencing in New York. In the back of my mind, I realized that some day I might be *him* (and if I'd had any sense of responsibility back then, I would have realized that that wouldn't be so bad); although, at that point in time, my childish dreams still refused to admit such a possibility. We talked about literature and philosophy. I proudly recounted the authors I'd been reading most lately: Don DeLillo, Thomas Pynchon, and Joyce Carol Oates. He nodded and agreed that they were all very good. Eventually, I said, "Mr. Hawthorn, it's been great talking to you, but I want to try to see Ms. Marlow before I go as well. Who knows when I'll get down here again," because Richmond was a place that, for me, held memories that, even by then, I never wanted to confront again.

"Sure. Sure. I'm sure she's still here. And next time you stop by, just call me Nate."

"Okay, I will."

"Good to see you."

"Good to see you, too." I almost added: "Nate", but I

didn't yet feel comfortable doing so.

"And, next time, let's meet up for drinks," he added, his intonation smiling, to my back as I returned to the memory-drenched hallways of my former high school. I wasn't quite sure if I was comfortable doing that yet either. But the thought soon disappeared as I drowned in the expanses of my own remembered (my stomach twisting at some of those remembrances) – no need to write it down – history.

The high school auditorium was already dark, the magic had vanished, rehearsals had ended for the day, the kids (I was certain) had drifted off to the James River – the rocks at Pony Pasture, the rope swing at Watkins Landing, to Maymont Park – the photo students used to take me there (other actors, as well) to model amid the grottoes and gazebos for their self-developed pictures, to the Virginia Museum in The Fan – small enough to learn, in one day, all the various periods of European art, and Ms. Marlow wasn't in there anymore. I needed to return to her classroom. But first, I needed to remember:

In the wings, where I'd spent so much time waiting, where I still dream about having never memorized my lines (I'm ready to go on-stage, but nobody told me the performance was coming so soon), there was a message scrawled in black magic marker: *In here, a frightened young mind was lost.* And it was... many times over. There were the seats where my mother and soon-to-be stepfather (never my actual father – he was driving two hours back and forth along the Pacific Coast Highway to his job in San Diego from his home in Laguna Beach that allowed him to never miss a child support payment and to fly me, lonely on the East Coast, out to see him at least twice a year to visit both him and the rest of one-half of *my* family) had sat, watching me – what had they thought of me as I played somebody else… so simply, so easily I stepped out of myself, a self that, for years (although I was unconscious of it back then), I'd never wanted to be. In those same seats, I remembered sitting side by side, while other scenes were rehearsed, with one of my co-stars, Ariel (she had come with me to Maymont Park to be photographed on many occasions), as we flirted and talked and held hands, and eventually, one day, kissed – my hand entangled in her blonde curls, our respective, nineties alternative-style clothing brushing against each other's: her, just a tad-bit hippie; me, a little punk rock. She'd told me she would never tell her children there was such a thing as Santa Claus; she would never shatter their little dreams like that – I wonder if she's stuck to that promise. But the purpose of this visit wasn't to remember, but rather to speak, to create (what I didn't know at the time) would become a new memory, would become: *this*, and I had to find Ms. Marlow.

Just as I'd suspected, she was in her classroom. There was a chair still set up in the middle of the room, left over from rehearsals earlier. I'd sat in that chair once. Leah and I had already broken up. I'd been going over my lines with a different co-star, Cora – the two of us alone. Cora had long black hair, black eyes, long hands, long fingers, long legs, and a long torso. She'd circled my chair as she'd said her lines, and with each rotation, she'd come closer and closer to me, staring into my eyes, delivering her lines straight to my mind. Eventually, I'd reached out and grabbed her. She'd agreed with my advances (I'd known she would – I've never been a particularly forward man) and settled into my lap, and we kissed there – underneath an imaginary spotlight. A few days later, I told her little sister (after I'd driven the fifteen year old girl out to the Shell station across the street to buy her cigarettes) that I was going to ask Cora to prom, but I never did. I never did. I'd wanted to. I'd thought she was so pretty, but instead of going with a drama girl from my own high school, I took another punk rock friend of mine from a different high school. We showed up late for prom, changing into our tuxedo and dress in the parking lot of a club in Shockoe Bottom after one of the local straight edge kids had pulled out a gun in order to stop the fight that had started between the band and his friends. Why didn't I go with Cora? She was so cool. We were in Creative Writing together. We had so much in common. She could have been my girlfriend... for real. My whole life would be different if I'd only taken Cora to my senior prom. At that moment, I wondered if Cora was part of that Richmond-New York connection as well... embarking upon the same artistic dreams that I was. Maybe I could find her in New York (I found out years later, via Facebook, that she wasn't there. She wanted to be, but she wasn't. Instead, at that point in time, she was still in Richmond, already a mother of two heading for her first divorce... I guess her life might have been different if I'd just asked her to senior prom as well).

"Well if it isn't my favorite, little Orestes: Matt Andrews," Ms. Marlow cried out as I strolled on in – a smile adorning my face, "What a pleasant surprise." She pried herself out from behind her desk and waddled her bulk over to me, arms outstretched for a hug. We embraced as only two respectful members of the theater world could, and she asked, "Where are you these days anyway? I haven't heard anything from you in years."

"New York," I answered.

"Doing?"

"Writing and acting, what else would you expect, Ms. Marlow?"

"Please, I'm Kris to you now."

"Okay, Kris, I live in New York."

"Really?" she responded, drawing out the vowels quite dramatically. I suddenly remembered what she'd always make us say during rehearsals when we had to do a part of our performance over again: *Thank you for this opportunity, Ms. Marlow.* Amid groans and grunts and disappointment, as groups of two, three, four, or five high school students heaved themselves off the floor of the stage, away from the proscenium and back to their starting points, the chorus: *Thank you for this opportunity, Ms. Marlow.* She went on: "You know, Kate Moore is up there as well."

"I know. She was the first person I moved in with when I showed up in the big, bad city. She gave me my first part in a show there." She introduced me to Evie, I didn't bother to add as I recalled the night that Evie and I had spent together, drunk on cheap wine and stoned on even cheaper marijuana. It was another night where I fell in love as soon as I held her in my arms in bed and she started to cry as she told me about her ex-boyfriend, her ex-fiancé, the talented rapper who, six months before, had suddenly died of an asthma attack. Nobody would ever hear his rhymes. They'd been dating since she was in college. Twenty-five years old… his whole career (a record deal had just been signed), his whole marriage, his whole life ahead of him. *What about his parents?* I'd wondered. But I didn't ask as Evie heaved drunken sobs. She was gone from New York, breaking my heart as life had broken hers… out to L.A., trying to find a place in Hollywood. I was certain I'd see her in a film someday. But I still remembered a conversation we'd had during the rehearsal of that show that Kate had directed:

"What's wrong with you today?" she'd wondered as I pouted outside of the Tisch Building while smoking a cigarette.

"Nothing, I just got another story rejected, that's all."

"Well, don't feel so bad about it, honey. At least it was just a story, at least you're not a woman going to auditions, being told you're

not pretty enough, that your legs aren't long enough, your breasts aren't big enough. You can always write another story, but I'm always going to look just the same." She shook her head.

But you are pretty enough, I'd wanted to say to her even though I never did.

"And Andrew's there – in Brooklyn. He got a book deal, you know."

"I know. He lives in Park Slope. I'm on the other side of Brooklyn, in Greenpoint. I just saw that play of his, the one that was in The Fringe Festival, the other week. We went out for coffee afterwards. He told me all about it: six figures for a first novel, not bad." And although I smiled when I said it, I didn't tell her the disappointment *I* felt, the shame *I* felt in the light of my one time friend's achievements. She might have noticed the burgeoning pain registering in my eyes, a pain that would only grow in the years to come (*I* was the one who was supposed to be famous, whose name everybody was supposed to know), the pain of jealousy and resentment, of anger and frustration: *Thank you for this opportunity, Ms. Marlow.*

As I had with Mr. Hawthorn, Ms. Marlow and I talked for quite some time... quite some time longer than I'd spoken with Mr. Hawthorn even. Today, I no longer remember much of that conversation (it was almost ten years ago... there were still two huge towers in downtown Manhattan, my generation of Americans had yet to have its members sweating through the sands of Iraq, I'd yet to see a journalist beheaded on the internet, the whole madness of the first decade of the 21st century hadn't occurred... yet), but I do remember one piece of that conversation very well: Quite full of my life in what seemed so far away in New York City, of my accomplishments since high school – graduating from a relatively intellectually prestigious college, working for a dot-com in Boston, and now an artist of sorts in New York, I said, quite flippantly, to Ms. Marlow, "Yeah, I don't get back to Richmond much these days."

But she didn't take that statement as lightly as I did. Looking a tad bit shocked, she responded, "Well, honey, you should. You've got *roots* here. One big taproot, right through *this* high school and into the heart of this city. And knowing your roots is damn important."

I didn't think much about it when she said it. Actually, I don't think I even believed her when she said it. She didn't know me as well as I'd thought she did, I figured. Hell, my roots ran from Richmond through Texas, back to LA and Chicago. But she was right. She spoke the truth. Truth is an abstract concept when viewed as a word; not so abstract when viewed as a sensation: *One big taproot, right into the heart of this city… Thank you for this opportunity, Ms. Marlow.*

Beetles

Burrowing into the brown sand, one beetle mounted another. I guess that's how they fuck. Unless, the one was eating the other. In which case, how different would that be, really? Two dogs, tongues lolling from the sides of their mouths, ran circles around one another through the distant brush. Both were females – neither mounted the other, though that's been known to happen. A man in a tank-top and a blonde woman in shorts walked the trail, talking. But neither of them would have thought of themselves as "man" or "woman". They would have said "a boy and a girl". Such is the way of the current generation.

From the tenor of their conversation, one could tell that they had been carrying on this dialogue through many similar walks. And in fact, they had. They'd discussed feminism, economics, and love across a multitude of comparable trails – even this one before. The dogs always ran in the distance beyond them, and the man and woman considered themselves friends. Their tongues had never touched. They'd never seen one another naked. That wouldn't happen until later, much later.

Not that at that point they hadn't already considered the possibility. It just didn't seem tenable. They were part of a tight-knit clique and each had dated the other's friends before. But some things are unavoidable, and just a little ways down the line...

On this particular occasion, however, as they rounded a corner in the trail and stepped over a remnant of somebody else's dog's shit, the woman, Sally, was telling the man, Jeffrey, "So I saw David the other day. He didn't say a word to me." She didn't seem particularly hurt either by this remark or by her ex's attitude. It was merely a statement.

But probing deeper, Jeffrey, with a tip of his sunglasses, nevertheless asked her, "Are you okay with that?" David was part of their tight-knit clique. Jeffrey knew the man well. Of all their friends, David was his least favorite. The man had an air of aloofness, and he had a tendency to laugh at the most inappropriate times. His green eyes gleamed wildly quite often, and Jeffrey thought that was merely an act, something he'd picked up from somebody else who had probably impressed him. Having moved to this small, mountain city little more than a year ago, Jeffrey was the most recent addition to the clique. He'd been added by a friend from another city who'd moved there the year before he had. She'd dated David as well (and even Jeffrey when he'd first moved there). Every woman in the clique had dated David, or at least, had had an awkward "good night" with him in his car. For the most part, David appeared reserved and socially awkward... evidenced by the miscommunications caused by the majority of his remarks.

"It was fine. He's fucking that girl, Joanna, now. What do I care? Do you know her?"

Jeffrey shook his head.

"She's friends with Rebecca who showed up at Melissa's party the other week."

Jeffrey nodded. He remembered that party. He'd been impressed with Rebecca. She had red hair, a full body, and a radiant smile. He thought that he needed to ask her out some time. Especially, since she wasn't really part of the clique. Meeting new people is always hard. Eventually, he did ask her out. She was quite nice, but she moved away shortly after his interaction with her. It was through no fault of his own, but even years later, he'd still get a little tingle when he thought of her. That was all before he got together with Sally, though. The tingle wasn't.

"I wish he could just be a normal person. You know?" Sally said. Jeffrey nodded. He didn't necessarily know, but sometimes it's better not to tell the truth. Besides, he got the gist of what Sally was saying. "I mean, he's so goddamn awkward. I ask him how he is, and he just says, 'Uh, about six foot four.'"

Jeffrey laughed. "He's a weird cat. That's for sure."

"Well, he's got his reasons," Sally added with a slight shake of her head. "I mean, there's a secret that nobody really knows about David, but I guess I've said too much already." She shook her head again – a little more forcefully this time.

Jeffrey was intrigued by her statement, but he didn't think it proper to pry. He'd learned over the years that the more disinterested you are the more likely you are to get the information you're seeking. If Sally wanted to tell him, she would. But while she didn't, a slew of thoughts spun through his mind. Was David impotent? Did he have a sexually transmitted disease? What precisely would a girlfriend know about somebody that the layperson wouldn't? A lot. Jeffrey had no answers. All he could do was let the conversation take its course.

Lost in his head, he almost stepped on a beetle whose ass was in the air as it burrowed into a hole that it was in the process of digging with its face. Jeffrey never liked stepping on bugs. He didn't like killing them. He didn't like hurting them. They were so harmless, and he had no respect for a person who felt the need to destroy the earth's lowest life forms (a bit presumptuous, perhaps), unless, of course, that person was protecting another person who had a fear of bugs. In the end, humans were still more important. Species politics were really quite interesting. They weren't so different from those on a grander scale. Nothing was so different from anything on any scale. Even beetles.

Suddenly, Jeffrey realized that Sally was still talking. How disappointed she might be if she'd known how far his thoughts had wandered, and that wouldn't have boded well for his forays into feminism – men never paid enough attention. They were too lost in their heads. Simone Weil had never said that, but Jeffrey believed it to be the truest complaint he'd heard women make against his sex. And, now, here he was…

Sally was saying, "…And there's lots of sex in it."

"In what?"

"*Rome*. Weren't you listening to me?"

Jeffrey couldn't do anything but shrug. He knew the TV show, or had heard about it, at least. But he'd never seen it. The train of conversation was lost. Whatever Sally had said was no different than the head of a dandelion blown by a child. It was a prisoner from her mind freed to oblivion, an outcast from Alcatraz who died swimming the San Francisco Bay. Jeffrey had to pay more attention from here on out.

While Jeffrey condemned himself, Sally took it all in stride. She was smiling at him shaking his head. "You know what I like about you?" she asked.

"No," Jeffrey said.

"At least you care."

He nodded at that; although, he wasn't quite sure what she meant. But it was better not to ask questions and just go with the flow. And right then, the flow was rushing in the direction of Sally's thoughts. "But while I was watching it the other night, I started thinking I should quit my job."

"Why's that?" Jeffrey asked – genuinely concerned, genuinely interested in what could lead to so drastic a life decision. Not that he knew Sally that well yet (if not her mind, at least her body, and bodies reveal a lot about minds), but he'd always imagined her as so together, so on top of things, the type of person who would wind up quite successful materially as she kept her priorities in order and did the next right thing. Obviously, he still had a lot to learn about Sally... but there was plenty of time for that. For now, it sounded as if his friend was, perhaps, not entirely happy.

"It didn't have anything to do with the show. That was just the moment in time. That's why I brought it up. But while I was making this necklace, I started thinking to myself – *Why do I want to spend all day sitting in a cubicle. I never imagined that for my life. I went to college because that's what my parents expected of me, and I went to a good school, an Ivy League school. But I don't like what I do. I'm not interested in what I do. Who cares about finance anyway? And in particular, who cares about selling financial products? Why don't I try to start my own business and just make jewelry for a living?*"

Jeffrey said, "I can respect that."

"I knew you'd be able to. That's why I brought it up. But tell me, how does somebody go about starting their own business?"

"I don't know," Jeffrey said, "But let me tell you, when I quit my job in New York, I knew I didn't want to write ad copy anymore. Oh, don't get me wrong, it was about the best I was going to do in the business world, but I knew I didn't want to *be* in the business world. So I moved out here instead. The rest, as they say, is history."

"Not very ancient history, though. But tell me, how did

you get the *courage* to leave a job like that in the city? I mean, what did you tell your family?"

"Well, luckily for me – and I don't mean this at all facetiously – my dad died a few years ago. So there wasn't anything to tell him. But that had a lot to do with why I quit. My dad spent his whole life trying to climb the corporate ladder, and all he ever talked about was how he was going to write a novel when he retired. But, you see, he never got the chance. Sure enough, he wound up damn successful eventually, but he never got to do what he really *wanted* to do. So when the opportunity presented itself..." Jeffrey tipped his head to the side and frowned to indicate, *You see,* "And my mom, well, she'd support me if I was checking condoms for holes in a Las Vegas brothel – as long as that was my dream."

"That would be a pretty funky dream," Sally laughed.

"There're definitely funkier ones," Jeffrey responded.

"Like George Clinton's."

Then, Jeffrey had to laugh, too. So there they were, walking down the trail, laughing at themselves, and for all intents and purposes really quite pleased – just thinking about the moment and enjoying one another's company.

"So you don't know that much about David, huh?" Sally suddenly said. She squinted and frowned.

"Nothing more than what's on the surface," which is all that we, as humans, ever really know about anything.

"Well, don't tell anybody about this. I probably shouldn't even tell you, but I'm going to because I know I can trust you and I figure you won't tell anybody else what I'm about to say."

Jeffrey nodded. He didn't know if he could be trusted. He didn't know if he wouldn't tell anybody, but sometimes we have to trust how others perceive us rather than how we perceive ourselves. We're busy measuring the effects with the measurement itself, and that's both impractical and insufficient. Any scientist would tell you that (speaking of trust) you couldn't trust the results of such a method. But is anybody else's perception more accurate? Aren't they merely measuring our effects from their own measurements? They have no idea how we are without their measurements affecting our system. We're all at a loss, floundering like a beetle with his ass in the air and his face in the dirt, attempting to make sense out of a world that merely makes no sense.

"See, this is what nobody knows about David." Sally paused and swallowed as if, even at this late moment, she were still contemplating whether or not she was going to say what she was going to say. Eventually, along with her decision, she nodded and told Jeffrey, "David has a kid."

That was certainly not the revelation Jeffrey had been waiting for. As a man, all he could think about was something regarding the other man's sexual performance. Taken back a bit, he drew his head into his neck and answered, "Really?"

"Really." Sally nodded again to emphasize her point. "And when I say you can't tell anybody, I mean anybody. Nobody else in the group knows. *He* wouldn't even tell me, and if anybody else found out, David would kill me."

"How'd you find out, then?"

"From his mom." In response to Jeffrey's confused gaze, Sally tipped her head to the side and went on, "Yeah, so this one day, when I was over at his mom's – David and I'd been dating about four or five months – I was helping her clean up after dinner when suddenly she said to me, 'See, I always told David that nobody would care he was a dad.'

"'Excuse me?' I said.

"*She* said, setting the plate she was washing to the side

and looking quite shocked, 'David never told you?'

"All I could think to do was kind of go with the flow and say, 'Oh, no, I didn't hear you. Yeah, you're right. It doesn't bother me at all.' I don't think she believed a word of it because I must have looked like I'd been hit by a truck. I mean, the only thing going through my mind was, *How can you sleep with somebody and keep something like* that *from them?* But that's David for you. I think, maybe, she knew David wouldn't tell me, and that was her way of getting me into the know. She's a really cool woman." Because parents, like always – even if Sally and Jeffrey weren't – *were* adults. "It must have taken me about four or five weeks before, finally, one day, David was complaining about people not telling him the truth and how he could see through them or some shit like that, and *I* said, 'Kind of like if somebody didn't tell their girlfriend that they had a kid.'

"Well, that sent him into a total tizzy. 'Who told you that? *Who told you that?*' He started shouting at me. When I finally told him it was his mom, and that *she* figured he would have already said something, he calmed down a little, and then he told me the whole story."

Now, Jeffrey was interested. He couldn't wait to hear the whole story, but still he stuck to his principles and didn't pry. Before too long, as they rounded a curve in the trail, while the dogs ran circles around one another in the distance, the whole story is exactly what he got. It came bursting out of Sally – word tumbling over word – as if she'd been waiting her whole life, and not just a few months, to tell it.

"Now, you may have heard that David was in a rehab a few years back…"

"I did hear something…"

But Sally didn't wait for him to finish. As if time itself were running out on them, she went on, "Well, you see, he met this girl there. Nowadays, he says, and get this, she was looking for a sperm donor. That's *seriously* how he looks at it." Sally shook her head, "David's so fucked up." Jeffrey shook his head along with her.

"So anyways, I guess they got together in this rehab. Then, they got together again after they got out. She told him she was on the pill so they didn't need to use any protection. Now, I don't know about you, but some girl or guy I met in a rehab, I'd be using protection…" Jeffrey indicated his agreement with a nod. Not that he had much experience with rehabs or even much experience with the types of people who went to rehab. Sure, he'd known a few, but none of them were really very close. Still, a nod seemed appropriate at that point in time because he was relatively certain that if he ever were to go to rehab, and if at that mythically horrific point in time, he were to get together with somebody, he'd use protection. Then, he wondered whether or not he'd ever gotten together with somebody who'd been in a rehab. And he hoped that if he had, he'd used protection. Then, he remembered that, both for her benefit and his, he'd better pay more attention to what Sally had to say.

"I mean, what kind of *jackass* doesn't use protection with a girl that he hardly knows? Whatever, as you can imagine, badda-bing-badda-boom, the girl got pregnant. But here's where it gets really tricky. You see, David wanted her to have an abortion, but she wanted to keep the kid, and she *promised* him that she'd never ask him for anything…"

"I see the sperm donor point, then," Jeffrey interjected.

Sally smiled in a manner that a nineteenth century novel might have called "coquettishly" at him, "But, you see, she *did* ask him for something. After she had the kid, she came to him for child support payments. He reminded her of her promise, and without even flinching she asked him whether or not he wanted to get the courts involved. Of course, he didn't. He knew the kid was his and any blood test would merely confirm what they both already knew. So there he was... fresh out of rehab, with a kid, and suddenly in need of a job to make those payments." Sally shook her head, "He never even sees the kid now – he's so angry at its mom. The only tie between that kid and his father is that David's mother goes over to visit him once a month. What a shitty deal, huh?"

"For David or the kid?"

"Both. Truth is, it all makes me feel bad for David, though, jerk that he might be."

"I don't know. Life certainly doesn't go the way we want it to, and things happen. I'm just grateful as hell that *I've* never gotten anybody pregnant. But if I did, well, I'd hope she'd have the abortion, and if she didn't, then..." he tipped his head to the side in the same manner as he had earlier when talking about his father's death.

Understanding his silent action completely (perhaps the reason that they eventually got together), Sally nodded. "But you can see why David's so goddamn weird. He's got so many fucking trust issues... especially when it comes to women..."

"Yeah, but that's his deal. *He's* got to realize that in the real world there aren't archetypes. Everybody's an individual, and, well..." Without warning, Jeffrey's attention shifted. He pointed down at the ground. "Look at those beetles..." he said, "This is, like, the hundredth time I've seen them doing that. What is it? Burrowing, fighting, or fucking?"

Original Face

In nothing but his underwear, Samuel sat down to meditate.
Behind his mind, his room was a schizophrenic mess.
Clothes were piled on shoes were piled on papers were
piled on book bags... He ignored it all and focused on the
tiny little corner in front of the exit where he'd brushed all
the madness away from. He sat down on his bedspread
(which was actually a sleeping bag since he didn't have a
comforter) on the floor since he didn't have a carpet or a
meditation mat for that matter. On top of the bedspread,
between his butt and it, were the two pillows from his bed
since he most certainly didn't have anything resembling an
actual meditation pillow. He criss-crossed his legs in the
lotus position and set one hand on top of the other –
palms up, thumbs touching. He focused his eyes on the
base of the wall where it met with the floor and relaxed his
gaze. After taking three deep breaths, he rocked his body
seven times from side to side to get his spine properly
aligned. He made sure his butt jutted out a little bit and that
he kept his neck straight. He didn't count his breaths
anymore, and that was okay.

As he skimmed the surface of his mind, the koan he'd
just read floated murkily upon it. With a psychic net, he
lifted it off the pond and brought it closer to his mental
eyes for examination (his physical eyes had already gone out

of focus; the world was turning dark). He didn't trust the translation, but he garnered a meaning still, which was exactly what he was supposed to be attempting at that point in his studies. Besides, he needed something only to delve deeper into, not a precise definition. Koans had layers upon layers to be exposed, and he dove straight into the deep end with that one. Three possible initial meanings: one – there is so much world out there that why should one limit oneself by convention (an invitation to swim deeper still); two – there are so many ways to be formal in such a wide world that the formalities one expresses may not be any more proper than the way one initially appeared; three – we are always formal... that is the key to our original face. What does it mean to have an original face?

A face before we were born? Samuel's face before he was born was one of three things: nonexistence, the same face he wore right at that moment, or the face of the world that had created him and that still created him. In a flash, he realized all three were right. So... what was his face right at that moment? That was a piece of what had created him and what still created him, and in that way, it was the key to nonexistence. Nonexistence was the key to everything because everything did not exist, at least, not in the way that people wanted it to, namely, essentially. It did exist precisely in that his face right at that moment had existed even before he was born as a piece of what gave birth to him. The moments after his birth formed his birth as much as the moments before his birth. The mistake was how one looked at time. Who ever taught you that time was linear? Who ever taught you that if it wasn't, then it had to be circular? Break the geometric bonds of your mind to break out of time.

Once time is abandoned, all of cyclic existence disappears. It could be said that the individual who is free of time has returned to that mystical Garden of Eden to eat from the tree of life... no longer plagued by the knowledge of good and evil – Nirvana is obtained. Of course, though, all mythology is as restrictive as geometry. There's no reason to believe that there is any psychological truth to a tale told by a human being. That was Freud's mistake. Presupposing an objective truth in a myth simultaneously presupposes something like Jung's Collective Unconscious. That's as erroneous as presupposing God. And He's the one who didn't want us to eat from that tree in the first place and become like Him. But for the record, we aren't paying any attention to mythology anymore. That would be limiting oneself by convention.

Earlier that night, a woman had read Samuel's face (before he was born?). He'd been at a pool hall – not drinking, just hanging out with friends and shooting a game every now and again. "You have an amazing way with the opposite sex," a female friend of his had told him after a woman unknown to him had introduced herself and carried on a long conversation – in between sips off her whiskey sour – about her best friend who lived in the Bay Area ("I thought it was close to San Francisco, but with the traffic, it's really not"). He'd shrugged. What could he say to such a complement? "I don't think I'd handle having that much power over the opposite sex as well as you do..." his friend had gone on.

"I never noticed that I had any power," he'd responded. "Women just like me."

"Regardless, you're a real ladies' man," she'd said.

"I guess," had been his answer. "I'm certainly not a man's man." They'd both laughed at that one.

"Did I introduce you to my boss yet?" his friend asked him next.

"Yeah…"

"She's pretty?"

"I thought so."

"I want to fix you guys up."

He shrugged again.

"Where'd she go anyways?" his friend asked. "I can't lose her."

"I'll find her," Samuel responded as he set his pool cue back into the rack on the wall and went in search of the lost boss.

He found her in a corner of the pool room talking to a woman with penetrating, black eyes. The two were thickly engrossed in a heavy conversation. Above the music (at that moment, The Ramones) he could catch snippets of their shared words, but he couldn't make out the details of what was being discussed. He tapped the boss on her shoulder. Expectantly, she looked up at him. "Remember me?" he asked. "We just met."

"Of course I do," she said.

He felt a bit awkward intruding upon the conversation, but there were no hints that he should leave. Leaning against a table, he merely waited for the moment of his introduction. With his proximity, however, he was better able to make out the state of their minds. The woman with the penetrating eyes was saying, "…And you need to pay more attention to men." She looked at him. "Like this one, he's got really nice eyes."

"She's telling me my future," the boss confided in him. That piqued Samuel's interest.

The penetrating woman went on, "See the color, the sheen of them. He's…" she trailed off and stared at him for a moment. She shook her head, "Anyways. You need to stop messing around with women and find yourself a man. You will have children. You will have a daughter, and she will bring you great pain."

"Oh, that's wonderful," the boss chuckled.

"Yes. But her father will love her and bring her comfort. She will do wonderful things, but you will not," the woman said.

The boss laughed. "So I'm just going to be this ho-hum person bringing a politician or something into the world who's going to break my heart. Great…"

"I'm sorry," the woman said. "It's just what I see. I can't help what I see."

Samuel smiled along with the mood of the two. His eyes widened, and his lips pointed up at their tips. The penetrating woman glanced at him. She smiled right back at him. "You, on the other hand, are quite wicked," she said – quickly adding, "But not in a bad way."

"No. That seems true," he agreed. As if it were a tractor-beam from a sci-fi movie, her energy pulled him closer to her. He wasn't sure if it did or not, but his physical presence may have actually invaded her proximity. Her eyes were black as the hole at the center of the Milky Way. Like the morning star with the sun, he spun into a spiritual orbit around her. A light lit in the depths of her pupils – the point of collapsed gravity at the center of the black hole.

The light manifested still more tangibly in her words, "You've been through a lot," she said. "You've suffered a lot," her building frown quickly exchanged places with a smile, "But that's okay. We all have, and you are okay. You will be okay. You will be married… in about five years. And you will have a son first. You will name him after yourself – as all men wish to do. You will accomplish what you wish to accomplish. You will…" her smile grew still broader. "You will…" she stopped in mid-sentence. "You have a powerful energy. I'm proud to meet you," she said. She put her hand out for him to shake. He enveloped it with his own. She wrapped her other small palm over the back of his hand. "I don't mean to see these things, I just do."

"That's okay," Samuel said, "I've seen lots of things I didn't want to," but he didn't stop smiling as his memories would have caused him to do a few years before that precise moment.

"Do you have children?" the boss suddenly interjected, directing her question at the woman with black eyes.

"I have three sons," she said. "My oldest is 20. I had him at fourteen. My husband is right over there." She nodded in the direction of a stout man with black hair who held a pool cue in his hand. "He's wonderful," she said, "But he's so unpredictable. We've been together since before my first child was born. He's a fire fighter, and I'm blind to him. I'm blind to him and to my children. I can't see anything for them. It's only with other people. I see auras."

"You're blinded by love," our hero added.

The woman with black eyes shrugged. She didn't seem to agree, and Samuel realized he was nowhere near as perceptive as she was. But he'd never imagined himself to be so. His gifts were otherwise.

"Everybody has psychic powers," the woman went on. Samuel nodded. He most definitely agreed with that. He'd had his own experiences, but there was no need to go into them right then. Instead, with the benefit of her words and presence, he could feel them building inside his mind. It was time for him to sit still. As if she were marking him for all time, the woman dug her thumb nail into the back of Samuel's hand. He didn't cry out. He didn't make any response whatsoever. He pretended as if nothing strange in any manner had just happened. "It was very nice to meet you…"

Samuel walked away from the encounter to return to his

friend who thought he was a real ladies' man. She was now shooting her own game of pool. She asked him if he'd found her boss. He nodded.

His thoughts were getting to be a bit too much, and he stepped outside the pool hall for a cigarette. Waiting outside, sitting on top of a low-lying brick wall, was the woman with black eyes. As if he'd already been invited to a secret rendezvous, an assignation designated by mysterious symbols – which he very well might have been, he hopped up next to her and lit a smoke. She was already smoking a cigarette so he didn't offer her one.

"I hope I didn't scare you," she said.

He shook his head, *No*. Then, he tipped his head to the side, *But what did you do to me?*

"I just feel such a powerful energy coming off from you. I didn't say this in there, but you have to be careful. You will accomplish what you want to, but something will eventually stop you." She stared at him. "I don't want to scare you. You already know what that is."

He nodded.

"It's so strange. I feel you pulling my energy from me..."

I'm a vampire... he psychically whispered to her.

"Stop it," she said. Then, "I'm sorry. I don't mean to freak you out."

"Oh... I've seen much freakier than this," he told her.

And as he said it, the unpredictable man who she'd nodded to as her husband approached the two of them. "What the hell are you doing talking to my woman!" he shouted at our hero, getting up in his face. Then, his tension relaxed, and he grinned, "Just kidding." Looking at the penetrating woman, he said, "Come on, baby, let's go."

But before the unpredictable man's snarl turned to a

smile, our hero had already unknowingly stuck out his hand and said to nobody in particular, "I'm Gabriel." As the two of them walked down the street – the unpredictable man putting his arm around the woman with the penetrating eyes and pulling her close to him – our hero whispered it, as if he wasn't quite sure, again, "I'm Gabriel..."

Warts

I got sober for the first time five years ago. Shortly after getting sober, I noticed a strange mark on the heel of my foot. I had no idea how long it had been there – I'd been in such a haze for so long, and I had no idea what it was. However, since it didn't hurt, I paid it no mind.

This mark remained on my heel throughout my five year stint of sobriety. It grew in size and shape, changed in color, and still I paid it no mind, particularly since I had never heard of cancer of the heel.

Don't get me wrong, every once in a while, when a case of athlete's foot that I appear to have picked up in one of the shower stalls of one of the homeless shelters that I've stayed in would act up, I'd buy a can of Tinactin and spray both my toes (where the athlete's foot was) and the mark on my heel with its white powder. The symptoms of athlete's foot would go away, but the mark on my heel would remain.

Six months ago, I wound up on the streets again, and eventually, I wound up picking up a drink and a crack rock again (actually, I picked up the crack rock first – the drink was just to help me pass out when the high wore off). In a certain respect, the whole fiasco was through no fault of my own. See, in addition to being an alcoholic and a drug addict, I'm also diagnosed bipolar with psychotic features.

Due to the nature of psychosis, in certain respects, this particular brand of bipolar disorder is more akin to its categorical cousin: schizophrenia, than to its own sibling: regular bipolar disorder (otherwise known simply as manic depression).

I say that in a "certain" respect, this fiasco was through no fault of my own because in another respect, it was entirely my fault. You see, although I did everything I could to combat my alcoholism and drug addiction, I honestly believed that if I just stayed clean and sober, I would never wind up in psychosis again. Obviously, that didn't happen.

I was getting my medication from overseas (it costs $500 a month here in the States), and it appears that I received a bad batch from my pharmacy in Mumbai. This may not have been a big deal, but, you see, I also have a very busy life right now (or, at least, six months ago I had a very busy life), and when I first felt myself losing my grip on reality, I remember thinking: *I just don't have* time *to go into a psych ward right now. I've got too much to do.* What I didn't realize was that I certainly had the time to spend a week in a psych ward getting my medications worked out, rather than spending three months on the streets getting beaten up, smoking up, drinking up, and almost waking up dead countless numbers of times.

I lost my apartment, lost my job, lost my girlfriend, and almost lost all my friends. I've been living at my mother's now for the past three months, and I really just want to get back to New York City and forget this whole mess.

But every event leaves its scars.

After I came off the streets, I noticed, on my finger, a wart. I figured I'd picked this up sometime over the summer of homelessness, but I had no idea when since, again, my world had become a haze. Back home, however, I didn't have any money, didn't have any insurance, and didn't know about any of the free clinics in town yet. The only way I knew to get rid of the wart was to go to the drugstore down the street and get my mom to buy me whatever over-the-counter remedy was available. It's pretty embarrassing to be 33 and asking your mom to pay for medication for a wart.

(But I also remember, after I came off the streets this last time, when she gave me a $20 bill and told me to go into Arby's and buy myself a sandwich… I looked at that board of food, and I felt the bill all balled up in my hand. And tears sprouted at the corners of my eyes as I thought to myself: *I can buy anything on that menu. There's nothing on that menu that I can't afford right now.* I ordered my food, the man brought it to me, and I said to myself: *The only thing that will ever feel better than this is when I've worked for the money that can pay for the sandwich that will make the pain in my belly go away.*)

While I was perusing my various options: wart-sticks, wart-freezers, wart-acids, and reading their respective directions of application, I noticed, on the back of one of the packages a description of an external Plantar wart. This description seemed to describe precisely the mark that had been growing on the back of my heel since I'd first gotten sober five years before.

But I'll tell you what, over my time on the streets, that mark on my heel had become disgusting. It had grown and turned black. It was thick, and when I touched it, finally, it hurt… In my psychosis, I'd thought it was a case of leprosy beginning, and that I would carry this leprosy with me through all eternity. I was Pazuzu: Lord of the Eastern Winds, Lord of All Fevers and Plagues. Jesus couldn't heal me. I was that which caused what he healed. I'd leave my possessions, not out of respect for him or his father, but only of my own volition. I was a very polite demon.

Reading the medical description of a Plantar wart,

however, I realized that I didn't have leprosy; I wasn't a
demon; I wasn't Pazuzu… I simply had an untreated wart
that wasn't going to be removed by Tinactin, but that just
might be able to be taken care of with some of the
medications available to me at Rite-Aid.

My mom bought me the wart-stick. I started applying it
to the wart on my finger and to what, I assumed, was the
Plantar wart on my heel. Layer after layer of skin peeled
away, but after two months of wearing a band-aid, neither
of the warts – not even the small one on my finger – had
completely disappeared. In fact, they'd hardly been affected.

One of the guys who works on the construction crew
I'm with (I'm a philosopher by training – even have the
papers to prove it) finally asked me what the hell was wrong
with my finger that I kept wearing that goddamn
bandage… I'd had it on since he'd first met me. "It's a
wart," I said.

"Well, why haven't you gotten rid of it?" he asked me.

"I'm using a wart-stick," I said, "It's just taking forever."

"Well, Jesus Christ, of course it is. Why don't you go to
the pharmacy, spend fifteen bucks, and just freeze that shit
off."

In all honesty, I hadn't thought of that. Fifteen bucks
had seemed like a million dollars when I'd first gone into
that Rite-Aid. My mom was already paying $500 to get me a
medication that would make it so that I wouldn't go
traipsing off into the wilderness… or into a gutter as the
case (with the postmodern world) may be. An extra fifteen
dollars, rather than the two that the wart-stick cost, just
seemed like too much to ask for. But I finally had a job; I
finally had the money. The guy I worked with was right.
The next day, I went out and bought the wart freezer.

God, it burned when I touched it to my already
stripped away skin. And it came with this acid solution that

I was supposed to apply for two weeks, and then, if the wart still wasn't gone, I could freeze it again (given the size of the wart on my heel, I'd bought the box that said: "For large warts").

I've been using this acid now and freezing the warts for a month. But last night, when I got out of the shower, I finally scrubbed my finger really hard with the towel, and guess what: The wart on my finger is gone. For the first time in three months, I don't have to walk around with a band-aid wrapped around my ring finger… where most men my age wear a wedding band.

Oh, the wart on my heel is still there, but it's little more than a thin layer of disgustingness covering a red, wounded portion of skin. And it stings when I walk on it. It burns, and when I'm not wearing shoes, I walk on my toes on my right foot. But I've got my band-aids (it takes three of them just to cover it up), and, in a pair of shoes, I can hardly feel it. In all honesty, I'm pretty sure that it'll be cleared up after one more freezing. I'm getting my medication directly from the manufacturer now. The doctor at the free clinic hooked me up with that. I still have to use Tinactin every once in a while, but some things, you just have to live with. Hopefully, next month, I'll have enough money to get back to New York City.

Once Upon a Time

We're so different, the young man realized he had always been taught as he read the myths of the primitive people: stories of worm holes and strings... things that a modern mind could never imagine were actually the case. He glanced up from the thought-meld he was experiencing and wondered if his world weren't the fairy tale he'd been taught their world was, if his world weren't merely a stringy worm crawling through a non-existent hole. Perhaps, that primitive world of wars and deceits, of science and technology were true. Perhaps, his world was nothing but a lie, something made up by the powers that be merely in order to keep him in line. Perhaps, it didn't exist – the figment of another's mind.

If that other world were to be, who and how could its creator be, and in what manner? As the young man contemplated that, he realized that he could never know. He could never actually imagine a world other than the one he had experienced and was still. All thoughts would be predicated upon his previous existence. He needed to learn how to expand his mind. He needed those drugs that he'd read about in the history books, the ones that fools had used not to stabilize themselves but to destabilize what they perceived as subject and object. That was the problem, everything was too stable. One needed an unstable equilibrium in order to fall. One needed to fall in order to grow. He remembered that myth, too, arising from an even deeper world.

Or maybe that myth had never been. Maybe that one was his own. Maybe that was the world he could create. He didn't yet know how to actually create a world. It was merely a thought. *I'll call myself God*, he contemplated in his own language… God being the only actual English word of that sentence, of this whole story, in fact. This whole story could be meaningless except for that one word. *And all the creatures of that world will bow down and worship me. They shall put no other gods before me. I'll love them so much that I'll even sacrifice my only begotten son for them… Well, tell me that isn't a manifestation of my own psychology, a mere abandonment complex. In other words: "I hate you; don't leave me." I need to come to terms with my parents' divorce. Still, it sure sounds nice, and my world will be better than this one. There, the people will know that they have freewill. None of this questioning, I'll simply tell them everything they need to know through revelation.*

Now, the only problem was: how did one go about creating an actual world? Should it be done with thought or matter or a combination of both? He'd start with a thing called spirit. That would form the fundament. Upon spirit he could build matter. Upon matter, he could build thought. He took a deep breath. As he exhaled, he realized that was spirit: the breath that gave birth to his words. Spirit would be the pure form out of which he could speak such sentences as: *Let there be light.* He did so, and there was light. And light was a form of matter because it could be seen regardless of the arbitrary divisions the ancient scientists might have wanted to make. And with light came plants. And with plants came oxygen. And with oxygen came animals. And with animals came thought. And with thought came evolution. And with evolution all this could come to be. There, he had created a tautological reality.

There was a sun shining outside his window right then. Its rays refracted through the glass and blinded a corner of his eye. As far as he could remember, it had been shining before he'd spoken as well. There was electricity flowing through his dwelling's veins. It buzzed through the light fixture above his head. That, too, had been buzzing before he'd spoken. He had to wonder: had he actually created the light he saw, or had something else? It was a strange thought, but maybe the world actually began that moment he realized what spirit was for the world he was going to create. Maybe, once he breathed out after that thought, the foundation of his own existence had been laid, and his words had been the words that had breathed life into the universe he himself inhabited. Maybe, prior to that, all that had been had been a dream. Maybe, he was his own creator as well as his father's and mother's and grandfather's and grandmother's and so on *ad infinitum*. Maybe, he really was that God he'd imagined himself to be.

So this was the world he had created. It wasn't such a bad world. He could imagine other worlds, but this was his world; obviously, the world that he had wanted to be. But if he had wanted this world to be, why did he still live with his parents? Why was he still in school? Why didn't he have a girlfriend? The only answer was that the greater Him wanted it to be that way. Someday, he would merge with that greater Him, and he would ask Him: why didn't I make me happy? And He would answer that question, and he would view his world from his Higher Self's perspective. That was something worth striving for. He would do so through contemplation and meditation and self-inquiry and examination. He would explore all internal regions in order to discover how his internal regions had created his outer regions because his thoughts had preceded his matter even though he'd just made it so that matter preceded all thought. He was not spirit. He was real. He was the inversion of his falsified world.

As soon as he discovered those means of exploring his internal regions, he would hand down those means through revelation as well. If his creations could recognize their true selves, they would realize that they were nothing other than Him. They, too, could merge back with their higher selves, which were the creators of this world as well. But he certainly didn't want there to be multiple creators. And if this were his world, then he could logically step outside that trap and create a new one for all those other higher selves to step right into. They'd snag their ankles in the trap's teeth, and they'd wait there, bleeding and crying for him to arrive to chop off their heads, leaving them unable to think anymore, leaving them unable to challenge him.

In order to find them in that trap, in order to chop off their heads, those higher selves must have to be none other than his Higher Self swallowing the ultimate existence of all other Higher Selves. But if his Higher Self was swallowing other Higher Selves, what kept another Higher Self from ultimately swallowing him, never allowing him to know the answer to that question: *why didn't I make me happy*?

All higher selves had to be his Higher Self because his Higher Self had exhaled that first breath, and through that first breath all had come to be including him, which meant that he had merely discovered Himself through his thought process. If his thought process led to the one ultimate truth of Himself, then all other thought processes would eventually lead to that same ultimate truth regardless of what type of machinations it might take to get there. Therefore, the means of awakening his universe (and getting out of his parents' house and dropping out of school and finally winding up with a girlfriend) was to get his universe to go through the same transformations he had gone through. When all pieces of himself recognized themselves for what they were, then he would finally be his Higher Self in actuality. He would be all. He was certain of it. He, and all else, would be All.

But as All, all would also be nothing because when All is, then nothing is as well. He was certain of that, too. Nothing was everything because without an object for the subject, then only one is. As he'd learned in composition class the other day, when making an outline, in order to have an A, you had to have a B. Without B, there's no A. He was willing to be nothing. Nothing was better than something if something meant he had to live with his parents and go to school and not have a girlfriend. Instead, if he were All, if he were nothing, then he would force his creations to sacrifice their girlfriends to him. He would own all life, and he could choose whoever he wanted for a lover. With that selfish motivation, how did he intend to wake up his creations?

He remembered an ancient movie he'd seen once where a guy had amnesia and would tattoo messages to himself all over his body in order to help him remember who he'd been the day before. That was what he had to do. He had to tattoo messages across himself. And himself was the visible world. He would call those messages art. And art would be defined as anything that his creations did: science, philosophy, painting, mathematics, literature, technology, dance, advertising, theater, etc. Therefore, every single thing that his creations did would be another piece of the puzzle reminding them of their true nature as Him. But first he had to remind himself. He needed to start the ball rolling. He couldn't paint. He couldn't play music. But he could write. He would write everything he possibly could. That way, he would never forget either this moment or the moments following.

He pulled a notebook out of his desk drawer. He picked a pen up off the desk. He licked the ballpoint, and he set its inky point down on the ruled paper. He wrote: *The...*

Catatonia

The figure embodied does not love but itself; time running backwards makes a lot more sense. He repositioned himself on the pillow on the floor on which he was sitting and continued contemplating his notions of mind. A story's reality is not the trajectory. Rather, the trajectory is our reality. He cocked his head at an angle and stared out the café window. The woman sitting beside him on the floor stifled a mild laugh at the book she was reading. His book was set aside. How did he know that woman?

There'd been a time, not too long before, when they'd made love. He was certain of it. They'd shared a bed. She'd nestled her head into his shoulder and rib cage, and she'd felt so perfect there. As far as he'd been concerned, they could have slept that way for forever. But time is not so kind. They hadn't slept in that comfortable position for quite a while. In the interim – eternities, perhaps – others had been nestled into his enclaves, and she'd nestled into others. Or had that all happened before? Such is the way of the modern world, and even that term had finally changed. Future shock: nothing remained the same for longer than a day… the question was: How does one define the length of a day?

Oh sure, we think it's the amount of time it takes for the earth to rotate on its axis so that we see sun then moon then sun again. But there are other dimensions, other worlds where a day might not be defined in such a way. He'd traveled to some of those other worlds. They were fascinating places.

There was one world where the sun never shone once. He'd spent the entire time in an airport waiting room, days and days and days spent waiting to fly away. Staring out the window, walking in circles, a multitude of others waited along with him. One guy would leave every once in a while, but he always came back. He said he couldn't find anything. Was that him? Still, the plane never arrived. Instead, our hero walked to the edge of the universe and jumped off. Somehow, he'd landed smack dab in the middle of this body in the middle of this café in the middle of... where the hell was he?

But he had memories. Even though he'd never been there before, he had memories. He remembered this woman with long, blonde hair sitting beside him who was stifling her mellow laugh. She had long legs that wrapped around his waist and neck in such a pleasant way. Too bad those were only memories. He wished he'd actually experienced that... He thought as he caught a glimpse of her out of the corner of his eye.

Did they know each other? Did she have a name that he could call to mind? Did he have a name that she could call to mind? Did he have a mind that he could call a name? Did she have a... Things were really getting quite complicated. It was time to take another sip of tea. Maybe, that would do.

The tea wasn't liquor, though, and liquor was what he really wanted. Maybe, he should stand up, step outside that café, and go to a bar. Did that strange place have bars? Was alcohol legal there? He might have stumbled into prohibition. There'd been a club named that in his hometown, and a *Star Trek* episode where something like that had actually happened. How did he remember all that? This town certainly was not a club (there was no strobe light hanging down from the sky, and the sun's mood lighting was all off for dancing), and he definitely didn't believe in science fiction. Life was too much like fantasy, and fantasy was reality, which was certainly science but definitely not fiction. He didn't think.

Fiction had too many rules, too many opinions and theories for him to take them seriously. A plot should progress from this point to that along a certain conceptual arc with definite points along the line where events of immense significance happen. But life was more like mathematics than that. Waiting only to be designated with any sort of significance, there were an infinite number of points along any given line. Art couldn't be written. It could only be lived. So why was there a notebook open in front of him? Why were there words on that page? What the hell had he been writing?

Maybe it was a mathematical equation, something algebraic with variables, something about time and existence symbolically represented as a short story. A short story… being one level of a building, a level less than ten feet tall, something that a giant may have to duck to get into. He didn't want to write things that giants had to duck to get into. He wanted to write things that giants could comfortably stretch out in, take off their shoes, and wiggle their toes through the carpet of. He wanted to write something that could accommodate a thousand giants, something like a second, which encompasses all eternity. What the hell was he writing? He'd lost his train of thought. The train of his brain, a brain trained… Wasn't that what they'd been trying to do to him, train his brain?

He'd always waited for the caboose as a child. Was that

in this existence or another one entirely? In whichever existence, he and his mother had played a game where one of them had to guess the color. The one who won got... well, the one who won didn't get anything. They were just playing. But that was certainly a feat of some sort of mental gymnastics: to assume what might be based on past experiences that somehow had happened, that somehow were still contained within the brain. What was the brain? It had a physical location. It could be pointed to with Cartesian coordinates, but did its thoughts exist physically or... What else was there beyond the physical, he thought as he glanced again at the long-legged woman sitting beside him.

One day, eventually, the train game he'd played with his mother had gotten boring because all the cabooses were green even though his story books told him they were red. Who had lied to him? Was his brain seeing what was red as green, or had they actually changed the color? Which was true, the story or what he saw? According to science, the story had to accord with reality. Could a giant really stretch out in something like that? If life rearranged the story, then the story became the history of science and life became the present of science, and the present of science was sometimes studied by philosophy. A philosophy of science itself had evolved nonetheless. He didn't believe in the philosophy of anything. It had nothing to do with the word's etymology. Nobody paid attention to etymology anymore... if they ever had – besides Joyce, of course. But he might have just been playing a game, an etymological game. Could one play a game with something as abstract as language? Was English malleable enough to still be childlike and play, or had it developed along with the stiff upper lip of its progenitors into an adult's post-industrial, post-colonial, postmodern poster child nightmare?

Did they even speak English here? What if he opened his mouth and all that came out was gibberish that only he understood... That's all that ever came out anyways, or so he thought. Then, he realized that everybody could understand whatever he said whatever world he was in. English was the universal language, just like French and German and Sanskrit and Chinese, but English was what he understood when he spoke it. He was the universe. That solved the problem most definitely. What need was there to be understood so long as he knew what he was saying? Did communication ever extend beyond the individual, the universe...

He turned, with a lovely smile, to wonder of the blonde sitting beside him, "What's so funny?"

Portrait by PJ Adams

About the Author

Michael Anthony Adams, Jr. is originally from Whittier, CA. He holds a master's degree in Philosophy from the New School for Social Research in New York City. As a teenager, he was the lead vocalist and lyricist for Richmond, VA-based hardcore band Broken Chains of Segregation. In 2012, he began publishing his collected works under the pen name Israfel Sivad. He's the founder of Ursprung Collective, a spoken word/music project referred to as "fantastic brain food" on ReverbNation. He was the primary lyricist on indie rock group One & the Many's first two albums, *Forms* and *Hours*. His writing has appeared in the *Santa Fe Literary Review*, *The Stray Branch*, *Badlands Literary Journal*, and more. He currently lives with his partner and collaborator, artist PJ Adams, and their children in Baltimore, MD.

www.MichaelAnthonyAdamsJr.com